IMPERFECT MATCH

MW00915132

USA TODAY BESTSELLING AUTHOR

MELANIE HARLOW

NEW YORK TIMES BESTSELLING AUTHOR

CORINNE MICHAELS

Imperfect Match
Copyright © 2018 by Melanie Harlow and Corinne Michaels

All rights reserved. Without limiting the rights under copyright reserved above, no part of this publication may be reproduced, stored in or introduced into retrieval system, or transmitted, in any form, or by any means (electronic, mechanical, photocopying, recording, or otherwise) without the prior written permission of both the copyright owner and the above publisher of this book.

This is a work of fiction. Names, characters, places, brands, media, and incidents are either the products of the author's imagination or are used fictitiously. The author acknowledges the trademarked status and trademark owners of various products referenced in this work of fiction, which have been used without permission. The publication/use of these trademarks is not authorized, associated with, or sponsored by the trademark owners.

Cover Photography: Nicole Ashley Photography
Cover Design: Sommer Stein, Perfect Pear Creative
Editing: Nancy Smay, Evident Ink
Proofing: Michele Ficht, Janice Owens
Paperback Formatting: Champagne Book Design

To Laurelin, for making this perfect match!
M & C

CHAPTER ONE

Willow

"I'M RETIRING," MY MOTHER SAYS AS I SIT IN THE CHAIR across from her. "And I'm thinking of selling the business."

"You're what?" I stare over the desk at her in complete shock. "Mom, you can't be serious."

"It's time, Willow. Your dad and I want to travel the world while we still have the energy to do it."

"Okay, fine, but don't sell the business! My Heart's Desire is the number one matchmaking service in Chicago! You've spent twenty years of your life building it up." My mother is brilliant and has this innate ability to see a couple's potential without any explanation. It's like she sees through all the pretenses and lies, and gets to the heart of what a person really needs.

She sighs. "I know, darling, but I'm not getting any younger, and you're not getting any better at this."

It's the truth, but I feel like I have to defend myself anyway. "I'm still in training."

"Willow, it's been three years."

"It takes *time* to make a perfect match!"

"I had five marriages under my belt in my first year."

"Well … I've come close a few times, haven't I?" I don't actually know if this is true, but I like to think it is. I've set up countless clients, followed all of my mother's directions. I've agonized over finding the subtle nuances in interviews that I think a client would appreciate … but all my matches have been total busts.

I'm clearly a love disaster where my mother is a guru—in work and in life.

"I suppose I could ask Aspen to take it over," she muses, looking out the window.

"Aspen!" My jaw drops. My mother cannot truly think this is a good idea. I love my sister, but she needs psychiatric help … or even just a shower and haircut. She took my parents' hippie mentality and decided it was a life choice, much like being vegan or keto. She feels that she can't partake in anything that supports the government. Therefore, she lives on my parents' land, steals—or borrows, if you ask her—their electricity, water, food, and anything else she needs. Then tries to say she's "living off the land." I called it being a lazy ass.

And then a month ago, my mother hired her at My Heart's Desire as an administrative assistant. In that short time, she's already made two matches!

"Well, if I'm not going to sell it, I need someone to take over. Aspen is so new at this—I was hoping it would be you. In fact, that was the entire point of you coming to work for me. With your business degree, plus my mentoring, I figured it wouldn't take long for you to be ready, but …" She gives me a pointed look as she trails off.

I sit up taller. "I am ready, Mom. Give me one more chance. I know I can find someone a perfect match."

She releases another heavy sigh. "And you know, I can't help but wish that out of all the people for whom I've found a soul mate, one of them could be you. I regret not finding *your* happily ever after. I'm positive that's your problem."

Here we go.

The fact that I'd rather be single than settle is a mystery to her. "It's not a problem, Mom. I'm happy. I don't currently need or want a man."

"You can lie to yourself, but not to me."

It's actually the truth. It's not that I don't believe in love, but I haven't been able to find it, and yet I'm very happy in my life. I live in a great apartment, I have the best across-the-hall neighbor ever (who also happens to be my best friend), I have plants to take care of, and no need whatsoever for another asshole boyfriend.

If there's a hole in my world, it's children. I grew up in the most insane, ridiculous home that ever existed, but I loved my childhood. We owned a beautiful lot up in Michigan with a freaking petting zoo. It was a time filled with new animals and trips out to the woods to search for buried treasure that my father hid the night before. It was sleeping under the stars, swimming in the lake, listening to ghost stories. (Later, it was my sister smoking plants that I'm sure my mother didn't know she was growing.)

I've always dreamed of children, marriage, and the picture-perfect happily ever after, with a little chaos thrown in.

The problem?

I have the worst taste in men *ever*. I'll think a guy is great, enjoy the first date, and then he asks for anal or something ridiculous on the second date and ... boom, single again. Yet another example of how much I suck at matchmaking ... I can't even find myself someone worthy of a second date.

But I've got a plan to get where I want to be. And while it doesn't require a husband, it *will* require me to have a job and an income. Seeing as I don't have another option lined up, I need to salvage this situation.

I try to redirect. "We're not talking about me, Mom. We're talking about the company."

"Fine, but is it too much to ask for a grandbaby before I'm in a wheelchair?"

"Mom, I'm thirty-two! You act like you're dying and I've failed to give you hope. Plus, we both know that Aspen will probably end up pregnant before me. Lord only knows what the hell goes on in that ridiculous Airstream she lives in."

My mother smiles wistfully. "Aspen is an old soul."

"And a hot mess," I grumble.

She mimics my words from a moment ago. "We're not talking about your sister, we're talking about you, my Weeping Willow. You could find love, but you have no prospects because you spend all your time with Reid."

My mother both loves and hates my best friend.

"I do not spend all my time with Reid."

"Really? Who were you with last weekend?"

"Reid and I had plans," I say with indignation. I don't know why that's a big deal. He needed help, and I wasn't busy.

"Okay, and what about Monday night? What did you do?"

I hate where this is going. "I was at home."

"Alone?"

"No."

She smiles with fake sweetness. "Who were you with?"

"I was watching television … with Reid." I tack the last part on softly.

"And the rest of the week? Did you have plans with friends?"

"I did, actually." Reid is a friend, so technically I'm not lying, right?

"Uh huh, and was the friend Reid?"

Damn her. "Yes, Mother. It was."

"And last night, were you busy with someone *other* than Reid?"

I glare at her because she knows damn well I was watching TV with Reid because that's what we do every Thursday. It's our thing.

"So to recap, you spent last weekend, Monday, Tuesday, Wednesday, and Thursday with him?"

My mother is a pain in my ass. A big one.

"Willow?" she nudges.

I roll my eyes. "Yes, okay? Yes, I spent all those evenings with Reid!"

"Did someone say my name?"

Speak of the devil and all that …

I groan and look back to see Reid Fortino himself standing in the doorway, looking like he owns the place. His dark brown hair is pushed to the side and he's wearing a very expensive black suit with a crisp blue shirt underneath, which makes his eyes appear even bluer. Broad shoulders with thick arms and a tapered waist make most women get all tongue-tied around him.

I like to tease him about looking like the male version of Xena the Warrior Princess—dark and brooding with that hint of danger … you're not sure if you want to run from him or maul him. Even though I have zero romantic feelings for Reid,

5

I can't deny how hot he is. He had a meeting today in the building and said if he finished early, he would stop by. I didn't realize what time it was.

Normally, I'd be happy to see him, but he always enjoys when my mother picks on me about my relationship status, and he loves to argue with her.

I look at the ceiling. "Really, God? Really? You couldn't have dropped anyone else at the door? It had to be him?"

"Which only proves my point," Mom gloats.

"What's up, Wills?" Reid asks, entering the office. "Were you talking about me or something?"

I straighten my head and look at him. "Yes, my mother was just saying that you're killing my love life."

He smirks. "I'm saving her, Mrs. Hayes. That's all. I keep the dirtbags away and—"

"And you keep the worthy ones from approaching," she says in her chastising-mother voice.

"You wound me." Reid clutches his chest.

Mom laughs with a shake of her head and I watch him charm her into submission. It's amazing and kind of scary to watch women around him. He's smooth, good looking, and has an ability to make even smart, strong women do his bidding. Well, all except me.

I'm completely immune to his charm, or as I call it, his bullshit.

"I doubt that very much, honey," my mother tells him. "If you're going to keep Willow from finding love, the least you could do is date her."

He nearly chokes and I burst out laughing. This might actually be fun for once. "He won't date me, Mom. He doesn't find me attractive."

"I never said—" Reid starts before getting interrupted.

"You don't think she's pretty?" Mom asks, as though he's a crazy person.

"I think she's beautiful." Reid looks to me for help.

Instead of bailing him out of what will surely be a painful conversation with my mother, I lean back in my chair with a shit-eating grin. *You're on your own, buddy.*

"Then why is the idea of dating her so terrible?" Mom presses.

"It's not." Reid loosens his tie.

"So you just want to monopolize her time but not allow her to find love?"

He opens his mouth, shaking his head but my mother is already on to her next question.

"You don't think she's worthy of finding love?"

"I didn't—"

"And what about the guys she does date, do you think it's okay to scare them off by walking around her apartment as though you live there?"

I nod. "Right, so unfair."

Reid glares at me with open hostility. Which makes me grin wider.

My mother folds her arms over her chest. "If you're not willing to date her, then you should at least allow her the opportunity to find someone else."

Reid struggles briefly for a reply, and then smiles like he's got it all figured out. "I know, Mrs. Hayes, but it's hard because Willow chases away the girls I bring home too."

Oh, that bastard.

He's so full of shit. First, he thinks what my mother does is total bullshit. Second, he doesn't even date; he just sleeps

7

with random bar girls and *calls* it dating. All he's doing is deflecting now, and when my mother turns to look at me, I can see it worked.

Damn it.

"Willow!"

He smiles triumphantly at me, and now it's my turn to glare. "I don't do that, Mom. I've tried to find him a nice girl, but he rejects them all."

My mother's gaze shifts back to him and I stick my tongue out at him, like the mature adult I am.

"It's just not true, Mrs. Hayes," Reid protests. "I *have* tried to find someone, but Wills is the reason all the girls say they can't love me. And I can't choose some stranger over my best friend. You understand, don't you?"

My mouth falls open because he just played her like a fiddle. My mother will never be able to resist his little wounded boy sob story. There's nothing she likes more than someone she can fix.

Drat.

"Oh, honey, I didn't know." She gets to her feet and pulls him into her arms.

Reid looks over her shoulder at me like the cat that ate the canary. "I've really struggled with this. You know, emotionally. I'm very sensitive that way."

For the love of God.

I flip him off as he tries to stifle his laughter. It almost looks like he's shaking with tears.

"Mom! You can't believe him, he's full of shit!"

Her arms drop and the disappointment in her eyes towards me only fuels my fire. "Willow Hayes, this man just showed a true bout of heartsickness over his desire to find love, and you chastise him?"

"You seriously don't believe that, do you?"

Reid covers his face with his hands.

"Oh, Reid." My mother says his name with a gasp. "I'm so sorry, honey."

And then he's fake-weeping in her arms again.

I'm going to kill him tonight. But how? I'm thinking food poisoning, since I've never known him to turn anything edible away. It would definitely be the easiest option and the least messy. Shooting him seems too bloody. And he's way too strong for me to choke, although the way he's grinning at me again might give me Herculean strength.

I move my mouth but don't make a sound. *I'm going to kill you.*

He smiles wider and mouths back, *I'd like to see you try.*

Game on, jackass.

CHAPTER TWO

Reid

WILLOW'S MOTHER ROCKS ME IN HER ARMS LIKE the sad, pathetic, unloved man I'm pretending to be. All the while, I'm looking at Wills and trying not to laugh.

She and I both know my act is total crap.

I'm not unloved or sad. She might say my inability to cook and shop for myself is pathetic, but as I remind her, she *enjoys* doing those things for me. I wouldn't want to take that away from her.

The truth is, I'm a normal guy with the best friend in the world living across the hall. She makes sure I'm fed, and she ensures I don't look like a total loser by helping me pick out clothes. More than that, she's always there for me.

When my dog died, Willow was there.

When my idiot brother Leo moved in because his girlfriend kicked him out, Willow helped make sure I didn't kill him.

When my ex-girlfriend cheated on me, Willow was the

one offering to help bury the body. (Glinda was not the good witch she pretended to be.)

There's nothing in this world I treasure more than our friendship.

Nothing.

Right now though, if looks could kill, she'd have murdered me six ways till Sunday.

"Come sit." Mrs. Hayes pulls me toward the chair.

Not wanting to let this charade die, I sniff as though I'm holding back tears.

Which earns me a major eye roll from Wills. "Oh, please," she says under her breath.

"I want you two to have someone in your lives to share more than just pizza and Chinese food with. You need a real relationship," Mrs. Hayes says while glancing back and forth between us. "I know you're friends, and it's so important to have that platonic affection too, but you need someone to love romantically who will love you back the same way." Before either of us can say anything, she lifts her hands. "Not that you two don't love each other, but you don't *love* love each other. I think we can all agree on that."

Willow sighs and nods, and she and I exchange a look.

No one gets our friendship. She's beautiful, not to mention funny, smart, and put together in that I'm-a-Real-Adult way, but it's never been romantic for us.

We've somehow managed to keep our friendship securely in the friend zone.

"My point is that maybe you guys are hurting each other instead of helping," her mother goes on.

"Mom, we're fine." Willow holds up her hands. "We really are. Reid is happy. I'm happy. Not everyone needs to be married to be happy."

Her mother turns to me with her best maternal stare. "Do you want a wife and children?"

The truth is no, I don't. I don't want any part of being a dad, or a husband, or turning into any version of my own father. I grew up with the most fucked-up parents a person could have. Mom is a raging alcoholic. Dad works constantly to avoid my drunk mom, and my brother and I had to fend for ourselves more often than not. They had all the money in the world, but they were miserable, and they made us miserable too. Why would I want to repeat that?

But I don't want to get into my fucked-up family history with Mrs. Hayes. I've barely talked to Willow about it. I prefer to leave it in the past where it belongs.

"I'm not sure I want a wife and kids," I say hesitantly, deciding to tack on another lie to avoid follow-up questions. "At least, not right now. Maybe in the distant future, if I met the right person."

Then she turns to Willow. "And you?"

"You know I want kids. Sooner rather than later."

"Then why don't you help each other? Or at least stop sabotaging each other?"

"What do you mean?" I ask.

"Let Willow try to find you a match, Reid."

"What?" My voice cracks in horror.

"We *are* a matchmaking service."

"Yes, but …"

Willow clears her throat. "Mom, you can't think this is a good—"

She continues on like neither of us protested. "Willow needs the chance to prove herself here, and you, Reid Fortino,

12

need someone who loves you enough to find you the perfect girl. What do you say?"

"Um …" I unbutton my collar, which suddenly feels too tight around my throat. "I'm not really—"

"I mean, neither of you is getting any younger," Mrs. Hayes points out, prompting Willow and I to exchange an eye roll. "I know women don't like to hear this, but there is a fertility window."

"*Mom.* Can we not discuss this right now?"

"Why not? It's a biological fact."

"I get it, and I already have a plan in place. You know that. In fact," she says, taking a breath, "I have an appointment at the clinic to discuss options."

My skin crawls. My hands curl into fists. If she wants kids, then great, I want that for her, but if she talks about artificial whatever-the-hell-it's-called one more time, I might puke. The thought of some weird asshole's *stuff* inside her makes me sick. What kind of pervy losers are jerking off in those clinics anyway?

"I support that plan, darling, but that doesn't help Reid with his co-dependency issues," her mother says. "He needs a match to cure his loneliness. And *you* need a romantic success story under your belt to give you the confidence you need to take this business to the next level, so *I* can sit on a beach in St. Croix and wait for news of the impending birth of my grandbaby." Mrs. Hayes beams beatifically, as if it all makes perfect sense.

I need to speak up, like right the fuck now. "Listen, Mrs. Hayes, I appreciate your concern for my loneliness, but there's no way in hell Willow is going to be able to find me a match. No sense getting her hopes up."

Willow sits up straighter in her chair and arches a brow at me. "And just what do you mean by that?"

"I mean that you're not going to be able to turn me into a romantic success story, Wills. And I don't want you to be disappointed."

Mrs. Hayes sucks in a breath and puts a hand over her heart. "I'm surprised at you, Reid Fortino. Willow needs us to believe in her. Are you saying she isn't good at her job?"

Damn. The woman is good. "No! I do believe in her. I just—"

"I'll do it." Willow stands up and gives me a defiant look. "I'll take you on." Then she aims the look at her mother. "And I'll prove to you that I *can* take over the business."

I raise my eyebrows. I can't tell if this is a joke, if I pissed her off too much and she's trying to get back at me, or if she honestly thinks she's going to be able to find my soul mate, as if such a thing exists.

"Wonderful." Mrs. Hayes clasps her hands at her chest. "Now let's have a group hug."

Willow comes over to us with a glint in her eye and the two of them hug me from opposite sides, while I stand there feeling like a piece of wood in a vise.

What the hell just happened?

"Are you crazy?" I ask Willow as I pull open the door of a cab. "Why would you tell your mother you can find me a match?"

"Mostly because you said it couldn't be done." She gives me a grin as she slides across the back seat. "I can't resist a chance to prove you wrong. It's too much fun. Plus you deserved it for feeding her that crap about how I chase away the girls you bring home. As if you give a shit about any of them."

Groaning, I get in next to her and shut the door. "This is not going to end well for you."

"Maybe, maybe not."

I give the driver the address of our building and sit back, giving Willow a pained look. "You've told me a million times that you're terrible at this. That your mom only hired you because her previous assistant quit unexpectedly and you'd just gotten fired."

"I didn't get fired, asshole," she says huffily, poking me in the leg. "I was let go because I refused to massage the data like the V.P wanted me to. I lost my job because I was honest."

"I know, I'm just giving you a hard time." Honestly, I'm glad she doesn't work for that finance company anymore. I met that dickhead V.P. a few times, and I'm positive the data wasn't the only thing he wanted her to massage. "You know I think you could be great at anything, including this romantic shit. I just don't need or want it."

"Methinks you doth protest too much, my friend. Maybe my mother is right about you, and behind all those walls you put up beats a heart that's longing to find its mate." She links her fingers beneath her chin and leans toward me, batting her lashes.

I put my hand over her face and push her away. "Quit it, you lunatic. You don't believe in that stuff any more than I do."

She laughs and straightens up. "It's not that I don't believe in it. I just don't have good romantic luck myself because all the guys I've dated have turned out to be dipshits."

"You can say that again," I mutter. Willow's taste in guys is beyond horrible.

"But this isn't about me. It's about you. And I know you well enough to find you the perfect girl." She nods slowly. "You know, the more I think about it, this is totally win-win for me. I prove myself to my mother and I get to have complete control over who you date for the next six months."

"Six months?" I gape at her.

"Duh, it takes time to find perfection," she says, like I'm a first grader. Then she toughens up her tone, pointing a finger at me. "And you better play nice. No fair sabotaging these dates or refusing to go."

I groan as my life starts to pass me by in a haze of terrible dates with desperate girls who have what my brother Leo calls an FFR—Face For Radio. "And what do I get in return for going through with this ridiculousness?"

"Everlasting love, of course." She flicks my shoulder.

"Not good enough. I want something from you."

"Like what?"

I think for a moment. "If I take this seriously, you have to promise me you're not going to let some jerk-off from the spank bank knock you up."

She sighs heavily and rolls her eyes. "One has nothing to do with the other, Reid."

"Doesn't matter. I think you're rushing into it and I want you to reconsider. I can't believe you didn't tell me you made an appointment." The cab pulls up in front of our building, and I swipe my card in the reader.

"I didn't tell you because I knew you'd throw a tantrum about it," she says as we get out of the car. "You've been weird ever since I told you about my plan."

I shut the door behind her. "It's the plan that's weird, not me. How can you think this is a good idea? You're completely

16

rational about every other thing in life." We walk together toward the entrance, and I pull open the heavy glass door to the lobby.

"This is absolutely a rational, not an emotional, decision," she says, giving me a pointed look over her shoulder. "*You're* the one getting emotional about it."

I try to think up an argument as we head for the elevators, but I can't. "You know that stuff about a window is bullshit," I finally say as she punches the up button. "Women are having babies later and later in life."

"It's not bullshit, actually. Age thirty-five is considered advanced maternal age, and a lot of women are having to resort to expensive fertility treatments to get pregnant. IVF with egg donors and all that. An IUI is a much more budget-friendly way to go." The elevator doors open, and after a few people exit, we step in.

The doors close and I turn to her. "What the fuck's an IUI?"

"An intrauterine insemination. It's the thing I told you about before."

"Where they let some creep who wanked into a cup knock you up with a turkey baster?"

She rolls her eyes. "Don't be so dramatic."

"I'm serious, Wills. You think Olympic athletes and rocket scientists are in there flogging the dolphin? Use your head. It's deadbeats and weirdos. Why am I the only one who cares about your baby's genetic makeup?"

The elevator dings at our floor and the door opens. "Fine, Reid. You agree to go at this match thing with an open mind, and I will put off my appointment at the fertility clinic."

"*And* rethink that plan," I add as we walk down the hall toward our apartments. "I can't even believe your mother is okay with it."

"My mother wants grandkids, and it's as clear to her as it is to me that it's not going to happen the usual way." She pulls her keys from her bag. "Why can't you just support me?"

"I can. I do. I just ..." How can I explain it to her without sounding like a possessive asshole? I'm not even sure why I hate the idea so much. I love Willow and I want her to be happy. If having a baby on her own will make her happy, why can't I just shut up and support her? We reach our doors, and I grab her arm before she puts her key in the lock. "Look, I'm sorry. But you know I can't keep my mouth shut when I have something to say, especially when it pertains to you."

She snorts. "True story."

"So do we have a deal? I go on some dates with whoever you choose and you hold off on the intergalactic insemination?"

A smile tugs her lips. "Intra*uterine* insemination."

"Whatever."

"Yes, we have a deal. But while you and the future Mrs. Fortino are planning your wedding, I will be moving forward at the fertility clinic, and I'll expect your full support."

My stomach heaves, but I hold out my hand and we shake on it.

Although there is no way in hell I am letting any of that shit go down.

CHAPTER THREE

Willow

H E SHOOK ON IT!
I sort of can't believe it. Reid can be mouthy and obnoxious and way too cocky for his own good, but I've never known him to break a promise or renege on a deal. Success—and a brand new purpose in life—would be mine.

All I have to do is find Reid a match.

"Hey, what are you doing later? You want to come over and watch Netflix or something? Get some food?" I ask him as I'm unlocking my door. The more time I can spend secretly probing his brain, the closer I'll be able to get to his ideal woman.

"Sure. I don't have any plans tonight."

I grin at him over my shoulder. "There's a shock."

He pokes me in the ribs. "Like your dance card is so full these days? When's the last time you even went on a date?"

"Why should I bother with dates when I have vodka and This Is Us right here at home? My night would end exactly the same, but this way I can cry on my couch without having to put on my skinny jeans first."

He shakes his head. "I am not watching any more of that show."

"Then I'm not feeding you. And you'll be sad because I'm making one of your favorites."

His eyes light up. "The ziti?"

"The ziti," I confirm.

"Damn." He frowns, and I can see him weighing a giant plateful of baked ziti against suffering through my favorite Friday night show. "Okay, fine. I'll come."

I give him a satisfied smile and opened my door. "I knew you would. Come over in an hour."

Scowling like a little boy, he grumbles something I don't catch, and I shut the door in his face.

I'm still smiling after I've changed out of my work clothes into plaid flannel pants and a big, sloppy gray sweatshirt. Nothing better than getting out of heels and a bra at the end of the day. I toss my hair into a messy bun and head for the kitchen, where I put the ziti together.

While I work, I put MSNBC on my iPad, which is propped on my cookbook easel, but I don't really pay attention to the news. I'm carefully cataloging everything I know about Reid Fortino, and trying to see him in a different light. A romantic light.

He's gorgeous—no denying that—and with my help, he's learned to dress better. I'll have to style him for his dates, but that's not a problem. He's got a great sense of humor (although he likes to make fun of me too much), so I definitely need to find him a girl who likes to laugh. He works quite a bit, but he's moving up the ladder at a trendy new marketing and PR firm, so she has to be understanding of his crazy work schedule. She'll also have to put up with the occasional client dinner—I've done a few of these when Reid needed a date on short notice with no expectations—but they aren't terrible. And it's kind of fun to watch Reid turn on the charm and go all "ad man" on prospective clients. He really is creative, persuasive, and smart.

As I layer the cooked pasta and meaty sauce into the baking dish, I consider his faults—the things any woman who's really looking for love is going to notice sooner or later.

First, he doesn't trust women. It's because he was burned so badly in the past. His parents are a train wreck, the absolute worst example of a marriage. And then, he thought maybe he could make it with his ex and ended up getting burned, which I get, but he's really got to put that behind him.

Second, he often doesn't think before he speaks, and it can get him into a shitload of trouble. Pair that with his healthy Italian temper, and you've got a recipe for disaster. Not that he has anger issues, but damn—his emotions run hot and close to the surface, and if you really say something to piss him off, watch out.

His favorite thing in the world to do is eat, so she's got to be a good cook, or at least willing to learn, because while he will happily make the drinks and do the dishes, he is beyond clueless in the kitchen.

There's only one thing about him that really baffles me. His love of comics. Not just comic books, though, but the entire world. I don't understand it. He goes to all those conventions, dresses in full costumes, and ... I can't even. But he's never happier than when he puts on some weird getup to go play with lightsabers in a tournament. He also knows it makes me roll my eyes so hard they hurt, which means he drags me to them at every opportunity.

Hence, three days a week I find the sappiest drama-ridden shows I can find and force him to sit and suffer through them.

But I suppose the biggest problem with finding him a match is that he's really fucking picky when it comes to women. I've suggested he take out a couple different friends of mine, but he always finds something wrong with them—either they're too shy or they won't shut up or they're just not his type. I'll have to dig deep tonight and figure out what that type really is.

I stick the ziti in the oven and set the timer for fifty-five minutes. After that, I straighten up my living room, water my plants, and throw in a load of laundry. I'm in the kitchen putting together a salad when Reid knocks three times and opens the door without my answering it.

"I brought you a present," he says, joining me in the kitchen. He sets a brown paper bag on the counter and pulls out a bottle of Tito's and a jar of fancy olives.

"Thanks!" I give him a big grin and pat his bicep. "But you still have to watch my show."

He groans. "If it didn't smell so good in here, I'd leave." Going over to the oven, he opens it and peeks in. "Mother of God, that looks amazing."

"When we find your future wife, I'll give her the recipe."

"Looks like you're going to be cooking for me the rest of our lives."

"Oh, ye of little faith." I'm going to find him a wife, if it's the last damn thing I do. He thought he was so funny today, but I'll get the last laugh. I get in his face and point a finger at him. "I bet you'll be married within a year."

"You're really cute when you're determined."

"Flattery will get you nowhere, my friend."

He laughs, grabs the jar of Tito's and my cocktail shaker. "You know, you were my favorite person in the world before today, when you sided with your mother on getting my wagon hitched."

"I'll be your favorite again when you're eating the ziti," I toss back.

"This is true."

He's so predictable. This is another thing I'll have to watch for. Reid is smart and he likes women who can keep up with his wit and sarcasm. Not only will she need to be pretty, but she has to challenge him.

I don't want to show it, but the task is starting to feel a bit daunting. Reid can be a pain in the ass, and finding someone to love him and put up with his shit is part one, but then finding someone *he* will put up with might prove impossible.

My mother is really evil for suggesting the idea.

"Do you want it dirty or straight up?" Reid asks.

"Dirty, please."

A few minutes later, he hands me a drink that's the perfect mix of vodka, dry vermouth, and olive juice, with four olives instead of the customary two, and I smile. "You're the best."

"I know."

"And so humble."

"I call it honest." Reid's smirk makes me want to slap him.

We both sit at the table, waiting for the food to cook, and I figure this is the best chance to talk about the whole match-making thing. I have a limited amount of time to find his dream girl and get them to fall in love. It occurs to me I might lose my best friend in the process, which makes me sad. I let out a heavy sigh, and run my finger around the stem of the glass.

"What's that face?" he asks. "Something wrong?"

I hate that he can read me so damn well. But I don't tell him what I'm really thinking. "Nope. Just thinking of what I can ask you so I'm sure to find that perfect girl."

"Oh, Jesus. Well, ask your questions already, so we can get this over with and I can eat in peace."

"And then watch an hour of beautiful storytelling in the most heartbreaking way."

He groans. "I regret this already."

"As you should."

I spend the next thirty minutes grilling him and enjoying every second of his torture.

》—♡→

The next day at work, I sit at my desk, sifting through the potential matches for Reid from the database of eligible females.

There's something wrong with *all* of them.

"Hmm, too tall."

"Too stupid."

"Too … blond."

I sigh and drop my face into my hands. I've been at this for four hours and I only have one maybe on the pile. He is seriously proving to be impossible to match. It doesn't help that the list of requisite traits he came up with last night was asinine. There is no way any girl will have a check in every box, but I have to at least find the majority checked or he'll toss her before she gets a chance.

Stupid, stubborn man.

I'm going to find another tearjerker show to torment him with because of all the grief this is putting me through.

"How's it going?" Mom asks.

I look up from the list with more red X's on it than circles, with a face that clearly says how much fun I'm not having.

"That good, I see."

"You couldn't have picked anyone else? Anyone? You had to assign me the man who has no desire to get married? All these women want to date someone who might actually propose someday. That's never gonna be Reid."

She smiles with that motherly look she's perfected and shrugs. "Life is full of challenges and I don't think Reid knows what he wants. He will when he finds her. You just have to bring her to him, which is what we do, Willow. We force people to open their horizons to ideas they don't think they believe in. Most of my clients couldn't find the right person not because they didn't want love, but because they weren't willing to truly open their eyes."

"Right, but Reid didn't come to us. You forced him on me."

"I gave him the option, and he walked through that door. He's ready for love, he's just afraid to take the risk."

"And you think I'm going to be able to show him the light?"

Mom smiles and nods. "I know you will. He'll see it."

My mother lives in a universe of eternal optimism. It's exhausting most days, but then, she's usually right, which makes it hard to argue with her. "Well, I need options and we are short on those."

"I have all the faith in the world that there's someone in our database for him."

"I'm glad one of us does," I mutter under my breath. "I'm leaving here in about five minutes. Reid and I are going to get him a few new outfits and then he's forcing me to go to the comic store."

"Life is all about compromise, darling."

"Like you do with Dad?"

She laughs through her nose. "No honey, that's twenty-plus years of marriage and knowing when to smile and nod. Men like to *think* they're important and have a say, when we all know the women are truly in charge."

"Good advice."

"I give it to all my clients after their weddings. Just like you can to Reid and his bride once you succeed."

Right. "Well, on that note. I should get going." I grab my purse and kiss my mother on the cheek.

"Have fun!" she calls as I walk out.

"Yeah, nothing says fun like the comic store!" I say as the door closes behind me.

On the elevator down, I shoot him a quick text reminding him that we're going shopping. He has stood me up one too many times for my liking.

Me: Meet me outside the store.
Reid: What store?

Oh my God. I knew it.

Me: Reid! We have a shopping date.
Reid: Who is this? I don't know this number.

I'm going to kill him.

Me: Funny. I'll see you in ten.

Reid: Seriously, stalking is a punishable crime. I request that you find another man for your attention.

Me: You realize I know where you live. Also, I feed you, and nothing says revenge like Ex-Lax.

Reid: Touché, my evil friend.

I huff and put my AirPods in as I stroll down the Chicago streets. It's so nice out today. It's beautiful for October, and I couldn't be happier. I have a cute fall sweater on, and with the sun, it feels at least ten degrees warmer than it probably is.

I think about each female face I pass on the sidewalk in a different way, wondering if she could be the one for him. I catalog their features, whether they smile as I pass, their height, weight, and overall stature. I keep hoping for lightning to strike, to find *that* girl. The one that will change his mind about marriage, open his eyes and his horizons, like my mother said. She has faith, so why shouldn't I?

Then Reid can get hitched, and I can get pregnant.

However, with each girl I study, I find something wrong. I start to question myself, and I wonder if I was being too hard on all the women in the database.

Why aren't they good enough to even show him? Why am I being so damn picky on his behalf? Maybe he'd like the tall girl. Maybe he will date someone who can't spell. Maybe I'm not giving him enough credit.

Before I can come to any conclusions, I plow into someone and nearly go over backward. "Shit! Sorry."

Reid's blue eyes meet mine as he catches me, and then his grin widens. "Wills. I always knew you'd try to fall at my feet."

"Yeah, that's it."

"You okay?" His hands are gripping my shoulders, keeping me from falling over, and I nod, straightening up.

"Yeah, I was in my head."

"Scary place that is."

"Not as scary as I was going to be if you didn't show."

He shakes his head and opens the large glass door of the department store. "After you, my lady."

"Thank you, kind sir." Delighted with his manners, I touch his arm as I walk past him and then he slaps me on the ass.

I give him a dirty look over my shoulder. "And they say chivalry is dead."

"That was for the Ex-Lax comment. Never threaten my food again."

I flip him off and decide to exact my revenge in other ways. After all, I control his dates for the next six months.

After an hour of Reid complaining as I pick out new clothes that don't consist of Spiderman T-shirts and track pants, we're finally done. I swear, he's the most difficult human on the planet some days.

We found some nice formal and casual clothes. The kind of first-impression outfits that women appreciate. No one wants to date a slob, which he's really not. He's just a little juvenile sometimes. I find it endearing and funny, but other girls might not.

"What are we doing tonight?" he asks as we walk out.

"Well, I'm working. I have to find your next hot date."

He groans under his breath. "Why do you hate me?"

"Because you'll need company when I have my baby—"

"Not by some douchebag with a turkey baster."

I huff. "When it happens, and I'm a mom, things will change for us. I don't hate you, I just want you to be happy too."

Reid starts to loosen his tie, which I know is a telltale sign that he's uncomfortable and doesn't want to talk about this, but maybe my mother was right. Maybe the two of us keep holding the other back because we're comfortable.

He's a great guy. He's everything that most women want, except maybe for the fact that he can't boil water and isn't very willing to share the remote, and yet he's alone. I know Glinda was a bitch in the end, but that was years ago. Since then, he's been dating the dumbest girls he can find so there's no danger of entering a real relationship, and the rest of his time he spends with me.

Lord knows I never want to admit my mother could be right, but ... I can see it.

"Things *will* change, Reid. We're both going to have to realize that and maybe it's time we grow up."

"I think we're pretty fucking grown up. And you and I both know I don't want a wife. I refuse to be my fucking father."

I bite my lip. It's so hard to watch him beat himself up over someone that he's *nothing* like. His father is cold and distant. Reid is warm and sweet. He cares about his family. He took his brother Leo in with no questions asked. I wish he wouldn't be so rough on himself.

"One day you're going to wake up and realize that you and Vince Fortino are not the same person."

"His blood is still mine."

I touch his arm, squeezing gently. "Reid, that may be true, but your heart is nothing like his."

"Glinda didn't think so."

Don't even get me started on that bitch. "She was an idiot. She's still an idiot, wherever she is."

He smiles and I see him trying to hide the hurt that lies under it all. "Maybe, but I can't fuck up a marriage like he did if I don't enter one."

"I've never known you to shy away from a risk."

"This isn't a risk, Willow. It's guaranteed failure. I'm not cut out for it. And why are you so anxious to get rid of me, all of a sudden?" He elbows me in the ribs.

"I'm not," I protest.

"Well, good. Because I like how things are. I don't want them to change. Do you?"

I'm not sure how to answer. In a way, I don't want things to change either. I've always known that if either of us finds *the one*, what we have will be gone. But thinking it could happen sooner rather than later is a little sad, even if it does mean reaching my goal of becoming a mom.

Because I love my time with Reid. I love our easy friendship and the way we have no expectations or demands. He is truly my best friend and if he gets married, he'll belong to someone else. And the baby I'm going to have will be my priority, instead of him.

But life has to move forward, doesn't it?

"Yes, Reid. I do want things to change," I admit. "I want to start the next phase of my life, raise a child, and have … something."

He stops walking and looks at me. "You do have something. You have us."

I look up into his blue eyes and touch his chest. "I have us. I know. You're my best friend, and I love you. Always will. And I want you by my side through everything. But …"

"But you want a Butterball."

"What?"

"A turkey-baster baby."

I sigh heavily. "This is why we can't ever have a serious conversation. You're an infant."

He pulls me close. "See? You don't need a kid, you got me."

I groan and bang my head against his chest, wishing I could magically transport to a place where men weren't so stupid.

Reid doesn't have to understand it, I just need him to support me. Hopefully, once I find him the love of his life, he won't give a crap about my baby-making parts.

This will be a win-win.

Won't it?

CHAPTER FOUR

Reid

"**S**O SHE'S GOING TO JUST SHOOT SOME SHIT UP HER vag and get a baby?" my idiot brother Leo asks on Sunday evening.

"I'm sure it's a little more in-depth than that."

Normally I'd never go to Leo about this, but Willow isn't around—she met some girlfriends for lunch, and then said she was going to the gym and to bed early.

So I'm stuck with this idiot for tonight.

"Why doesn't she do like all the girls did in high school? Tell her to get drunk, forget to take her birth control and call it a day. Boom. Baby."

"It's a wonder your girlfriend left you."

"I know, right?" He pushes his head to the side with a nod. "It's her loss."

Yeah, that's it. And my gain.

I was content living on my own, and I didn't want to deal with a damn roommate, let alone my brother. He drives me fucking crazy. He's lazy, he's a slob, and he can't even cook. I'm

32

sure the girls Willow picks are going to love having to adopt my brother along with dating me.

"Speaking of loss, do you have the money you seem to have misplaced?" I ask him.

He looks guilty. "About that …"

And another month I have to cover his end of the rent. "Leo," I groan.

"I'll have it. Soon."

"Not soon enough. I'm throwing you out."

He laughs because he knows I won't. Our parents are two people who never should've procreated. Leo and I only have each other to depend on, and some days I wonder if we'll ever get over the shit we grew up with. I thought I was done with it all when I walked away from my parents at age twenty-two. I gave up my rather large trust fund and never looked back.

Daddy Dearest was pissed that I didn't want to work for Fortino Hospitality Group, and he cut me off completely. Then he tried to groom Leo into taking my spot, but Leo hadn't spent his entire adolescence going to board meetings and shadowing Vince, as I had to call my father in the office. For all the things my brother is, an executive he is not. He was a trophy kid, if such a thing exists. Leo was a star pitcher, and he was supposed to do great things in athletics—but they drove him so hard, he burned out by high school. I was supposed to be a businessman, a second-generation power-hungry CEO. It was all about appearances.

I would've rather been poor and loved than deal with the pressure to be perfect. We could never live up.

Leo laughs. "You'd miss me if I were gone."

"Yeah, that's it." I roll my eyes. "I'd miss you like I'd miss the plague."

That's a lie, I like having him around sometimes. But what was supposed to be a few months has turned into a year, and in that time I've realized my little brother needs a lot more than just a place to live.

He needs guidance. He needs a decent haircut. He needs lessons on How to Adult. I like comics just as much as he does, but my wardrobe does not consist solely of jeans and faded Marvel T-shirts with holes in the armpits.

The one thing I envy about Leo is his job—I'd like to work at Midnight Comic too, doing nothing but hanging out and talking about comic books and graphic novels and other geeky shit all day. But no. I have a real job that makes real money so I can live in a real apartment and eat real food, even if Willow does have to cook it half the time.

I wonder what she made for dinner tonight. Leo and I are watching Swamp Thing and pigging out on pizza and breadsticks, but it's not nearly as good as Willow's ziti. Or her chili. Or this thing she makes with eggplant and tomatoes and rice that I thought was going to be disgusting (because eggs and plants do not go together on a plate) but was actually delicious.

I look at the slice of pizza I'm holding and can't bring myself to eat another bite. Maybe there's leftover ziti from Friday in Willow's fridge. Is she home from the gym yet?

"I'll be right back," I say to Leo, getting off the couch. "You don't have to pause it." Before leaving my place, I grab the spare key Willow gave me to hers. As I leave my apartment, I realize that I'm not going to hers only for food. I hope she's there. I miss her.

And that conversation we had yesterday is still bothering me a little bit. I don't like the idea of our lives moving forward in separate directions. Maybe it's selfish, but I kind of like having her all to myself.

I knock first, but there's no answer, so I let myself in. The living room lights are off, and it doesn't look like she's home. Snapping on the kitchen light, I go directly to the fridge and open it up, getting excited about what I might find. There's some healthy-looking green leafy stuff, something that looks like it might be chicken salad with grapes in it, and a white box that looks like it might contain her lunch leftovers. I open the lid and sniff—mmmm, lemon and garlic and artichokes over lightly breaded chicken.

Graciously leaving that for her in case she was planning to eat it for dinner tonight, I move things around until I see what I'm looking for—a plastic container of ziti. I recognize it because it's identical to the one she sent home with me Friday night, which Leo ate sometime after I went to bed despite the fact that I left a note on it that said LEO: DO NOT EAT.

I decide he doesn't deserve any more of it, so I pull the container from the fridge and grab a fork from her drawer. Without even bothering to warm it up, I lean back against her counter and dig in. Even cold, it's fucking delicious.

"Reid!"

I look up from the ziti in surprise and see Willow standing in the archway between the kitchen and living room wearing nothing but a towel, her hair dripping.

"Jesus, Wills! You scared me."

"You break into my apartment and *I* scared *you*?"

"Yes." I take another bite and try to keep my eyes in my head where they belong, but damn. I know it's Willow and we're just friends and all, but that towel is short and her legs are fantastic and the top of her boobs are sort of pushed up above her arms, which are folded across her chest. Plus she's wet. She'll have to forgive the stare.

And the twitch in my pants, if she saw it.

I try to covertly adjust myself. "I didn't think you were home. And I didn't break in—I used the key you gave me."

She gives me a flat, unamused look. "I gave you that key so you'd water my plants while I was on vacation."

"I know." I stuck another bite in my mouth and tried to concentrate on chewing it.

"You didn't do it. They all died."

"Oh yeah, that's right," I say with my mouth full. I point the fork in her direction. "You probably should have taken your key back right then."

She rolls her eyes. "I should have. Maybe I will. Didn't you eat dinner?"

"Leo and I ordered pizza but it sucks."

"So you just came over here to raid my fridge?" She taps her foot on the kitchen floor. Her toenails are painted bright red, which reminds me of the time I lost a bet—I can't even remember what it was about—and she made me paint them for her. I did a terrible job and complained the whole time even though her feet are small and kind of adorable. It wasn't really much of a punishment, to tell you the truth. In fact, standing here trying not to ogle her body in a towel might be worse torture. That twitch is now a full-blown erection.

"Yes, sorry. Were you planning to eat this for dinner? I left you the lemon chicken thing."

"How nice of you."

I shrug. "I'm a nice guy. How was the gym?"

"Fine." She turns around and walks out of the kitchen. "I have to get dressed."

"Why? It's not like I've never seen you naked."

She stops halfway to her bedroom door and looks at me over one shoulder, her mouth open in outrage. "What? You have not."

"Have too. That time we got drunk and jumped off the dock at your parents place in Michigan."

She whirls all the way around and faces me. "It was pitch dark that night! And I was wearing a bra and underwear!"

I consider that. "Maybe, but if I recall correctly, they were white. White doesn't hide much. And it sort of glows in the dark."

She huffs and crosses her arms even tighter over her chest. "You said you wouldn't look."

"I was drunk," I say. "You know you should never believe anything I say when I'm drunk."

The look she gave me could have singed the scruff on my face.

God, I love making her mad. It's so much fun and it's way too easy. I don't even know why I'm saying this shit right now—we don't usually flirt, but her body is making me all kinds of crazy, and the best thing for her to do would be to go put some damn clothes on before I remember how long it's been since I've had sex.

Instead she juts her chin. "Well, I saw you naked too."

"Oh yeah? When?"

"Same night. I was the only one who kept my underwear on. You jumped off that dock in your birthday suit."

"You were completely turned in the other direction."

She looks smug. "Not when you got out."

I have to think about that for a moment, but the memories of that night, beyond her perfect curves in white cotton and lace, have my brain a bit muddled. "I guess it's possible you saw me naked."

That makes her snort. "Oh, it's more than possible. I saw you."

"Why didn't you ever say anything?"

"Why didn't you?"

Setting the empty container and fork aside, I shrug. "I didn't want to make you uncomfortable."

"Ha! Since when?"

"I don't know. I guess I didn't want you to worry that I thought about you like that."

A few seconds tick by, during which I wonder what the actual fuck I am doing.

"But ... do you? Think about me like that?" Her voice has grown softer. More curious and less accusatory.

"Sometimes," I admit, and it's the truth, although a second later I want to kick myself. I should have lied. "But it's no big deal."

She blinks. "What?"

"I mean, I'm a dude. We're always thinking about beautiful women like that."

Her defenses go right back up. "So, what you're saying is, I'm not special."

"I'm not saying that at all. In fact, you're so special I shut down those kinds of thoughts about you right away. Because I don't want anything to ruin what we've got. But it doesn't mean I never have them."

"Oh. Okay." With that, she turns around again and walks away.

"Hey, wait a minute!" I chase her into the darkened living room and grab her by the elbow. "What about you?"

She looks back. "What about me?"

"Well,"—I struggle with words, which is odd for me—"do you ever think about me like that?"

Her eyes are wide and innocent. "Like what?"

"You know." Letting go of her arm, I make a forward-motion gesture with my hand. "Like when you saw me naked, did it make you *want* me?"

"Want you?" She tilts her head and squints a little, like she's thinking back. "No, not really."

I'm so stunned, I just stand there, jaw dropped.

She moves toward her bedroom again, and it's not until she starts giggling and breaks into a run that I realize she's fucking with me.

I take off after her again, reaching her door just as she tries to slam it shut. Without even thinking, I burst through it with so much force I crash into her and we both go down onto her bedroom floor. She's trapped beneath me, squealing with laughter and scrambling to get away, and I manage to get her wrists pinned over her head, snickering triumphantly. My body is sprawled over hers, that towel and my clothing the only barriers between us, and neither of them hides my hard-on very well.

Oh, fuck.

She stops struggling, and both of us stop laughing. Her breath is coming fast, her chest rising and falling rapidly beneath mine. My heart is beating way too hard.

The lamp on her nightstand is on, and her face is in the light. Her lips are open. Her eyes are locked on mine. Her expression is expectant—*what comes next?*

I recover my senses, that's what.

Letting go of her, I hop to my feet and nod once. "Let that be a lesson to you."

Then I'm *out*. I need the safety of two locked doors between us. I need a beer. I need a cold shower.

Jesus fucking Christ, that was close.

What the hell was I thinking?

CHAPTER FIVE

Willow

WHAT ... JUST HAPPENED?

I lie on my floor looking up at the ceiling for a solid five minutes, but my heart refuses to slow down. I can't seem to breathe normally. My stomach is tied in knots.

Propping myself up on my elbows, I try to piece together how I ended up on my bedroom floor with Reid on top of me, his *totally* obvious erection pressing into my thigh.

One second we were bantering in the usual way, making fun of each other and taking cheap shots, and the next he was barreling into my bedroom and throwing me down on the carpet. I tried to get away, mostly because it was fun to fight back, but he easily overpowered me—and then I felt his dick on my leg. And I saw the look in his eye. I was positive he was going to kiss me, and I suddenly felt this fluttery *thing* in my chest.

The fluttery thing happens again as I'm thinking about it, making me shiver.

Slowly, I get off the floor and sit on the edge of my bed, staring at the spot on the floor where we'd lain.

It would have been a mistake if he'd kissed me. No doubt about that. Reid and I are not that way. Oh, sure, we flirt here and there, but that's mostly just to get under each other's skin. Tease each other. Drive each other nuts. It isn't real.

Still.

There's something different about what had almost happened tonight. Taking a deep breath, I put my hand over my belly, and I swear I can feel the butterflies. Reid isn't supposed to give me butterflies. I never feel butterflies. I'm not a romantic when it comes to myself—too many horrible experiences with men have killed those instincts. My butterflies are dead, dammit. DEAD.

Rising, I hang up my towel and put on comfy underwear and pajamas, remaining in sort of a daze. I comb through my damp hair and put on moisturizer. I wander into the kitchen and heat up last night's chicken for dinner. While I eat, I watch an episode of This Is Us, but I can't even concentrate enough to get weepy.

When I'm done, I put my plate and Reid's plastic container in the dishwasher. I drop my fork into the silverware holder, and I'm about to stick Reid's in when I stop and stare at it instead. Then I bring it to my lips and close them around it before pulling it out again.

It's stupid. We've shared a fork before. We've shared water bottles, straws, tasted each other's drinks, dinners, desserts.

But this isn't that. It's something else.

Then I'm annoyed with myself.

"For God's sake, knock it off, Willow. Are you that hard up?" Disgusted, I throw the fork into the dishwasher and shut the door.

Ten minutes later, I'm lying in bed, eyes closed, trying to sleep. But those dang butterflies in my belly just won't quit.

Flopping onto my stomach, I try to smother them. Suffocate them. Send them back to the graveyard, where they belong.

Because it's really fucking bothersome that of all people, it was Reid who brought them back to life.

Another ten minutes pass.

Then twenty.

Then forty.

And another forty.

Now I'm getting pissed.

Screw him.

Who does he think he is? He can't waltz into *my* apartment, rummage through *my* fridge, and screw with *my* emotions.

I'm the victim here, dammit.

Throwing the blankets off, I hop up. I'm the one over here analyzing this crap, wondering why suddenly my best friend has me all … confused and whatnot. I put on my off-the-shoulder sweatshirt to cover my tank and some boy shorts to cover my underwear.

I have a key to Reid's place since Leo locks himself out constantly, so I grab it from my purse, dash across the hall, and stealthily let myself in.

I'm on a mission.

When his bedroom door flies open, he sits up in bed. "What the—?"

"You don't get to teach me a lesson," I say as I stand on the threshold of his room with my arms crossed.

"Wills?"

"You don't come over to my house and think that you can do … whatever it is you did just now, and then leave."

He starts to move off the bed. "What did I do?"

"You … you know."

"No, I don't." Reid takes a few steps toward me. He's wearing sweat pants, but he's bare-chested. "Why are you awake?"

"Because I can't sleep."

"Why can't you sleep?"

Because of you and that's stupid, right?

I can't say that, though.

Even in the darkness, that stupid feeling is in my stomach. I wanted it to go away. I hoped the anger and time that's passed would've ebbed because this is Reid. Reid, my stupid best friend who I cuddle on the couch with. The one who makes weird faces and eats my food. He's not the guy that makes my heart race.

He's never been that guy. Not even shirtless.

But right now, my chest is tight and my pulse is through the roof.

"I don't know, but …" I can't finish my sentence.

"I can't sleep either," he says.

"Well, it serves you right!" And then I wonder, is it because he's just as confused as I am?

"Why?"

Because I wanted you to kiss me. Because I stuck your stupid fork in my mouth, wondering what your lips would taste like on mine. Because I can't stop remembering how you felt against me.

Oh, God. Coming here was a bad idea.

Reid moves closer. "Why are we both up, Willow? Why do you think I can't sleep and neither can you?"

His chest is *right there*. He's so close, and I can smell the faint hint of musky soap from the shower he must've just taken. Our bodies are almost touching and I can't move. If something happens, it will be intentional, not because he got a glimpse of me naked.

This may have started as an anger thing, but it's clear that right now, it's all about desire.

"I don't know," I manage to say.

His finger pushes a piece of hair behind my ear. "Why did you come here?"

Why is he asking me this? Does he not see that we're both crazy and this is stupid and wrong?

Reid and I aren't attracted to each other. Not really. This is just some weird mood thing or maybe my sister put a hex on me for something I did. He and I aren't anything. I mean, we're not *this*.

I wish I could tell my body that. With him so close, it would be so easy to lean up, press my lips to his. We could just ... try.

"What are we doing?" I ask him, needing to make sense of my jumbled-up mind.

He looks down at me and shakes his head. "I don't know."

Neither do I, but I do know that this will change everything, and not in the way I've imagined. We won't be able to go back in time and be the friends we've always been. Sex could ruin everything.

I look up into Reid's blue eyes and know that I would

rather walk away now and have him as just a friend than ever know life without him. "I should go."

He nods. "But you never answered my first question. Why did you come here in the first place? Was there something you needed to tell me?"

I could tell him all the things I was feeling and he would understand, because he's that amazing, but I don't know that we could ever be the same again. This will pass—it has to, and then I'd regret ever opening my mouth to begin with.

So I lie. And I lie in a way that will break this spell we're both under. "To talk about the girl I found for your first date."

He takes a step back and my chest aches, but it's for the best. Whatever this is, it won't last. It's just the fact that I haven't gotten laid in so long, that's all. It's freaking Reid.

I'm clearly just wound too tight and he's the guy my libido has picked.

Makes perfect sense now that I've put it into perspective.

"Oh?" he asks before clearing his throat.

"Yes, I found a girl I think will be perfect and I meant to tell you earlier, but forgot. So, I was up racking my brain about what I forgot to tell you and came over here to do that … to tell you … about the girl."

"And it couldn't have waited until it wasn't midnight?" He asks moving farther away from me.

"Nope."

"I see."

"Good."

He nods. "Good. So what happens now? You set us up on our date?"

Date. Why does that word make me want to hurl right now?

"I'll call her tomorrow after you look at her profile and set it all up."

Reid sits on the end of the bed. "If that's really what you needed to tell me, I'm glad you can get some sleep now."

"Yeah, totally will. Whew," I say with a sigh and mock-wipe my forehead. "Thanks for letting me clear that up. Glad you were awake too."

His head moves up and down slowly. "Yeah, would've been awkward, you barging in here, if it weren't about something important."

"Right," I say and start to back out. "Okay. Goodnight."

"Goodnight. Sleep tight now that you've gotten your head cleared."

I smile. "I will. You too."

Yeah, like I'm going to sleep at all for the next week.

>—♡—→

"You look like hell," Aspen says as she enters my office Monday afternoon.

I really don't have the energy for my sister today. She requires full brainpower to comprehend, and I have maybe a quarter remaining. I'm so tired, confused, and emotional, I can barely think.

Not to mention she shouldn't talk about how I look. At least I match and don't have weeds hanging in my hair.

Aspen gives a whole new meaning to the words *flower child*. She literally has flowers in her hair, on her clothes, and believes their perfume is enough to mask anything.

They're not. Not even close.

"What are you doing here?" I ask her.

"Dad is visiting our madre and asked me to come along. He got me a few things for the compound."

"Aspen, it's not a compound, it's the backyard."

"It's where I'm in touch with the world." She's so far out of touch, it's not even funny. "What are you working on?"

"I'm finding a match for Reid."

She laughs. "Really?"

"Yes, why?"

Aspen comes closer to the desk. "Can I see your prospect?"

My sister is a lot like my mother. She sees things in people—I wish I had that gift, but I don't. They always talk about the eyes and how you can see a person's soul and truths. I think they're just eyes, but apparently this is why I suck at my job.

"No," she says as she hands me back the paper.

"No?"

"No. She won't work."

I sigh. "Why?" She's truly the best I've found. Each trait that Reid requires, Kandace has. She's pretty, smart, has her own money, she cooks, and she is even in the same field as him. Her video profile made me a tad bit ragey because she was so perfect for him.

"Because ... she's not for him."

"Aspen," I groan. "I need more than that."

"It's a feeling I have."

"You haven't even met her!"

Then my sister sits ... on the floor ... because my chairs are wood and she has a thing about trees and death. I don't point out that the floors are hardwood because I don't have the emotional capacity for that fight.

"I don't need to. Reid will never match with her."

God, give me strength.

"Well, I think you're wrong. She's got everything he wants."

"I would wager you're incorrect," she retorts. "In fact, I know you are, like you were when we were little about where the sun went as it set." Aspen smirks and tilts her head to the side.

When she does that, I'm instantly eight years old and want to pull her hair and call her names. My sister and I were the worst as little girls. My parents have a huge home. It's ridiculous, but they insisted that we share a room. They both grew up very modestly and believed the bonds with their siblings were strengthened by sharing.

So, Aspen, who's been a slob since she was little, shared my room.

My beloved room, which I'd color-coded for easy cleanup. I liked order and a bit of neatness, but my sister would purposely make the room a mess.

Making me … crazy.

We fought daily, calling names, pulling hair. We were so bad my parents finally separated us, but Aspen thought it was comical to still come into my room and destroy it.

Right now, I feel like she's doing the same damn thing.

"I wasn't wrong then and I'm not wrong now. You barely even know Reid; I know everything."

"Not who is right for him."

I groan. "I think I know what he's looking for more than you do. You looked at a photo."

"She has crazy eyes."

Now I've heard it all. "I have a crazy sister."

"Yes, but my eyes aren't."

Oh, I assure her, they are. Everything in front of me right now is. "Whatever, she's my best pick for him."

"Well, you're going to be sorely disappointed when he meets the crazy-eye girl and suddenly starts to second-guess you."

"If you're so smart, who would you pick?" I toss back at her. She thinks she's so good at this? Let's see *her* find someone for him.

Aspen closes her eyes, with her hands on her knees. "You."

And now I know she's really crazy because there's no way Reid and I could ever work. We're too different. Whatever chemistry the two of us felt last night was a fluke.

Tonight will prove that.

CHAPTER SIX

Willow

ONDAY NIGHTS ARE WHEN REID TORTURES ME with all of his comic book shows. They're so bad. I know he thinks my sappy shows are terrible, but at least the plotlines are decent.

His shows are meant for teenage boys, and apparently he still is one.

However, it's almost eight and he's usually here by five to eat whatever I have in the house.

Me: Where are you? Dinner is going to be cold.
Reid: I'm stuck at work.

Okay, and he didn't let me know? Weird.

Me: Are you leaving soon?
Reid: Yeah, getting my stuff now and I'll be there soon. What did you make?
Me: Food.

Reid: Well, good. Because food is my favorite thing.

I laugh. He personifies the typical saying about the way to a man's heart.

Me: Okay, I'll keep it warm. See you soon.
Reid: Don't leave me only a little either. I didn't eat lunch and I plan to lick the plate clean.

I'd like to lick ...
I slap myself. Literally. I can't believe I just let my brain go down that path. After my sister's comment, I'm trying not to think about him like that. It's insane to imagine I would be a match for him, and once she said it, it was as if my brain recognized the stupidity too.

We are perfectly matched as friends. That's it.

My perfect guy is nothing like him, and I don't really want a man anyway. I want a baby. I don't need a man to have a baby.

And Reid sure as hell doesn't want that with me. He doesn't want that at all.

He likes spontaneity, and I'm the furthest thing from that. I like order, plans, and follow-through. Schedules and lists.

We'd never work.

But for the next forty-five minutes, I can't stop myself from wondering what if ...

"Hey." Reid's voice fills the room and I jump.

"Hey. In the kitchen."

He walks in and I brace myself. I wait to see how my stupid body will react because my mind is already at peace, knowing I feel nothing.

Thank God, I don't feel anything weird. Just my normal affection for my best friend. Sure, I notice that his suit looks especially good on him today and that his blue tie makes his eye color deeper than usual. And so what if I like the fact that he must not have shaved this morning, giving him more scruff than usual? That doesn't mean anything other than I like guys that have scruff.

Reid walks over to the table, kisses my cheek and then grabs a roll that was on my plate. "How was your day, dear?"

I only need to say one thing. "Aspen helped me with your matches."

Reid's brows shoot up. "Oh, now I'm really excited for tonight."

"Hardy har har."

"Oh, come on, you know your sister is my favorite lunatic."

"She looked over all the girls I picked for you."

"Let me guess." His smile matches the excitement in his voice. "She hates them."

"Nope. She thinks one is really a winner."

He laughs. "Liar."

"Whatever."

"It's fine, Wills, we both know you're never going to match me, which means our evenings will remain quiet, without a screaming baby in the background. Just accept that our lives are meant to be this way."

"I get six months to change your mind, remember?"

Reid laughs and then opens the oven. "Did you make Dorito casserole?"

"Maybe."

"You know I love Dorito casserole."

"You love everything I make."

He nods. "This is true. I also love you."

I try really hard not to let that comment get to me. I know he's saying that he loves me as a friend. We both have said it countless times before, it just … feels different.

Stick to the plan, Willow. Find him a match.

"So I'm thinking one night this week will be perfect for you to invite Kandace for drinks after work," I tell him, poking at a tomato in my salad.

"Who the hell is Kandace?" he asks, his mouth full of the pilfered roll. He takes his suit coat off, hangs it on the back of a chair, and drops into the seat. There's another salad on the table in front of him, and he gestures to it. "Is this mine?"

"Yes. Kandace is your dream girl." I look him in the eye and smile sweetly. "Your perfect match."

He snorts. "Is this the one Aspen thinks is a winner?"

"It's the one *I* think is a winner." I stick the tomato in my mouth, although I'm suddenly not that hungry.

Reid sticks the rest of the roll in his mouth and sits back in the chair, arms folded across his chest. He chews and swallows, never taking his eyes off me. "You're really going to make me do this?"

"Yes. I think Thursday would be perfect," I go on, sticking my fork through a piece of lettuce on my plate. "Nothing too fancy, just a happy hour cocktail. If it goes well and you hit it off, you can ask her to dinner."

Exhaling heavily, he gets up, goes to my fridge, and takes out a bottle of ranch dressing. As he dumps giant blobs of it into his salad, he says, "I'm not asking her to dinner. One cocktail and I'm out."

"Don't be so negative," I scold. "You promised to go into this with an open mind and a good attitude. You have to at least try to be charming—although I know that's difficult for you."

He gives me a look as he sticks a bite of salad into his mouth. "And what do I get out of this again?"

"You mean aside from everlasting love and a soul mate for life?"

He rolls his eyes. "Yeah. Aside from that."

Laughing, I get up from the table and take the casserole from the oven. "You can be godfather to my intergalactic baby?"

"You'd trust me to give spiritual guidance to your child?"

I shrug as I set a trivet on the kitchen table and place the hot dish on top of it. "Why not? And if anything ever happened to me, you think I want Aspen raising my kid? Poor thing would probably go to school without shoes and never get a tetanus shot or see the dentist." I grab two large, shallow pasta bowls from the cupboard, and serve myself a small portion and Reid a massive slab of the casserole. When I finally sit down and pick up my fork, I notice he's staring at me silently.

"What?" I ask, disconcerted. "Is there something on my face?"

"You're serious about that."

"About what?"

"Naming me the godfather of your child."

I blink at him. "Of course I am. Does that surprise you?"

"Yes. No." He shakes his head. "I don't know … I guess I just picture a godfather as being, you know, an *adult*."

I have to laugh. "You are an adult, Reid."

"An adultier adult." He scratches his scruffy chin. "Someone with a lawn mower and a grill in the yard and a station wagon for Sunday drives. My car doesn't even have a back seat. And what if I forgot to feed it? Look what happened to your plants."

He looks so distressed, I can't even tease him—much. "Not even you could forget to feed a child. I promise. Kids let you know when they're hungry."

"But I don't know how to cook."

"I suppose you'd have to learn. Or hope that your wife knows."

"Oh, right—I forgot about her." Looking relieved, he digs into the crunchy topping of the casserole. "What's my wife's name again? The one for Thursday?"

"Kandace."

"Yeah. Kandace. Good old Kandy. Remind me to make sure she can cook. I can't let my intergalactic godbaby starve." He shoves a bite into his mouth. "What's she look like, anyway?"

"She's very pretty. I can show you a picture after dinner." I poke at my casserole while a small part of me wishes I'd chosen someone slightly less beautiful.

I'm not hungry at all anymore.

There's a weird lump of something in my stomach the next day when I pick up the phone to call Kandace McMillan. It's not dread, exactly—I have no reason to think this won't go well. After dinner last night, I showed Reid her profile and he agreed she was pretty and sounded interesting. "A hot physical therapist who enjoys baking, craft cocktails, and reading graphic novels?" He nodded enthusiastically. "I might actually like this one."

I stare at her photograph. *She's pretty, but is she really hot?* I wonder. I mean, she has freckles dusting her nose and cheeks, just like I do. I've always hated my freckles—the curse of fair skin. That's not hot, is it? And yes, she has long, thick, honey-colored hair, but maybe Aspen was right about her eyes. They do look a little glazed, although they're a stunning shade of blue. And her mouth is full and soft.

Without thinking, I pull a compact from my desk drawer and analyze my face. Are my brown eyes less alluring? Are my freckles more noticeable? More homely? Is my blond hair too ashy? I smile ghoulishly at my reflection. Are my teeth as white? As straight? Are my lips as plush and inviting? If they were, would he have kissed me the other night?

Angry with myself, I snap the compact shut and pick up the phone. *This isn't about you,* I tell myself. *Get a grip.*

Kandace doesn't answer, so I leave a message. "Hello, this is Willow from My Heart's Desire, and I'm thrilled to tell you I've found a fantastic potential match for you. He's a smart, funny, handsome ad executive, and he'd love to meet you for a drink Thursday after work. Can I set that up? Give me a call back and let me know. Hope you're having a great day!"

I end the call and set my phone down, noting that the lump has grown bigger. Determined to ignore it, I busy myself with other work tasks—clearing my email inbox, reviewing new profiles, checking on our social media ads. About an hour later, Kandace calls back.

"Wow, he sounds great," she gushes. "I'd love to meet him. What's his name?"

"Reid," I tell her, placing a hand over my belly, where that stupid blob of anxiety is still lodged. "Reid Fortino."

"Reid Fortino," she says dreamily, like she's already picturing herself signing checks as *Kandace Fortino*.

"Can you meet at The Darling at six?" I ask her, naming a quiet, classy place that's perfect for craft cocktails and conversation. "I'll make a reservation for you in the library there."

"Ooooh, I've been wanting to go there. Yes, that sounds perfect."

"Great. I'm sending you a link to his profile now, so you'll know him when you see him. He'll be sent yours as well."

"Thank you so much, Willow. I'm so excited." She giggles. "I haven't even met him yet and I've got a great feeling about this!"

"Me too," I say, and it isn't exactly a lie. I do have a great feeling about them. On paper, they're a perfect match. In person, I have no doubt they'll find each other attractive. She seems outgoing and genuine, and he'll probably charm the pants off her right from the get-go.

So why am I hoping Thursday never arrives?

CHAPTER SEVEN

Reid

"WHERE'S THAT WHITE SHIRT YOU BOUGHT on Saturday? The one I liked with the camel sweater." Willow rummages around in my closet while I watch from my bed.

"I don't know. I might not have even taken that stuff out of the bags yet." I'm lying on my side, one hand propped under my ear, trying not to stare. She's in a shitty mood today, but she looks adorable. She's wearing some kind of fuzzy sweater that's also a dress, and even though it's baggy as fuck, it's nice and short.

"Reid!" She turns around and parks her hands on her hips. "They're probably all wrinkled now."

"So I'll iron them. I've got almost two hours before I'm meeting what's-her-face." Ironing is the only domestic skill I have, but right now I really don't feel like doing anything but watch her stomp around my room, muttering to herself about what a hopeless case I am.

"Kandace, her name is Kandace."

I shrug because it doesn't really matter what her name is, it's not going to last past the first date anyway. So instead of arguing with Willow, I just go back to watching her. She's wearing these tall boots I like. They cover up a lot of her legs, but there's just enough thigh showing between the tops of the boots and the bottom of the dress to drive me a little crazy. When she finds the bags of new clothes in the corner of my room, she bends over to grab them, giving me an even better view.

I'm probably going to hell, but ever since Sunday night, when I tackled her in her bedroom, I haven't been able to stop thinking about getting my hands on her. And my mouth. And various other body parts. I've jerked off to the memory of us on the floor a stupid number of times since then.

My fantasies end differently though. Instead of coming to my senses and going home, I tear that towel off her with my teeth and fuck her senseless right there on the rug. I give her the best orgasm she's ever had, and I know it for a fact because afterward she says to me in this breathy voice, "Oh, Reid, that was the best orgasm I've ever had. Your dick is just amazing."

Alas. Real life is a little less sexy.

"Reid, you're not even listening to me!"

"I'm sorry, what?" I try to focus. Thinking about banging Willow is a terrible, horrible, no good, very bad idea. It can never happen.

"Plug in your iron," she demands, dumping the bags out on my bed. "I'm not sending you to your first date looking like you slept in your clothes."

Exhaling dramatically, I get up and pull an ironing board from the back of my closet. "Okay, Mom."

"Are your nice jeans clean? The dark ones without any rips?"

I set up the board and grab the iron off the shelf in my closet. "I think so."

"Good. Can you find them and make sure? If not, wear the charcoal pants."

I cock a brow at her over one shoulder. "Jeez Louise, you're bossy today, even for you. And why are you in such a bad mood?"

"I'm not," she snaps, shaking out a white button-up.

"Yes, you are. What's wrong?" I walk over to her, take the shirt from her hands and toss it on the bed. "Talk to me."

Sighing, she drops onto the bed and hangs her head. "I don't know. I've just been in a weird mood this week."

I sit down next to her. "Is it that time of the month?"

She gives me a searing look. "Fuck off."

"Okay, okay. Sorry. Bad joke." I hold up my hands. "But it's got to be something. I know you." I brush her hair back behind her shoulder. "Talk to me."

For a moment, she's silent, her eyes on the floor. "It's … it's just … it's the baby thing." She looks up at me like she just remembered why she'd been upset. "That's what it is. I saw something, um, a friend of mine posted. She's pregnant."

"Your friend is pregnant?"

"Yes. And it really bothered me, because, you know, I want to have a baby." She nods, like it makes perfect sense. "Yep, that's what's wrong." She tries to get up, but I put a hand on her leg and keep her where she is.

"Hey. Look at me."

Reluctantly, she meets my eyes. "What?"

"Is that really what's going on with you?"

She nods, pressing her lips together like she's scared words will escape.

"You're really serious about this baby thing, huh?"

Another nod.

I feel guilty all of a sudden that I haven't been more supportive. She does so much for me, and there's not much I can do for her. For fuck's sake, she's planning to make me godfather to her child. Me! I still can't believe it. It really means something that she has that kind of trust in me. In my judgment. Couldn't I offer her the same?

"I'll go with you to the clinic."

Her jaw drops. "What?"

"I'll go with you. To the basting place." I can't keep the grimace off my face, but I try to sound upbeat. "Maybe if I go and learn about the process, I'll feel better about it."

"Reid, do you mean it? Really?" The look on her face is pure joy. I feel kind of amazing I put it there.

"Sure."

"Thank you!" she squeals, throwing her arms around my neck. She comes at me with so much force, in fact, that she knocks me over backward. "Thank you, thank you, thank you!" And somehow we're horizontal again, chest to chest, only it's me trapped beneath her this time.

She picks up her head and looks down at me. Can she feel how fast and hard my heart is beating? For a moment, I feel like I can't breathe, like I'm suffocating, like there's not enough oxygen in the room and it's affecting my brain, which must be true because there's no other explanation for what I do next.

I kiss her.

I reach up, take her face in my hands, and lift my head so my lips meet hers.

She's startled, and I feel her little gasp. But she doesn't back off or get up or even tell me to stop, which is what I'm sort of hoping she does at this point, because clearly I am not thinking straight.

But neither is she. Instead of breaking it off, she tilts her head and kisses me back, pressing her mouth more firmly to mine. A tiny sound escapes the back of her throat—part sigh, part moan, part *what the hell are we doing*—and it turns me on so much I thread my fingers into her hair and kiss her harder, deeper.

I know it's wrong, but I can't stop.

I open my lips wider and stroke her tongue with mine, and she lets me. I tighten my fists in her hair, tilting her head back so I can kiss my way down her throat, and she lets me. I taste her skin, breathe her in, and it's familiar because it's Willow, but it's also crazy weird because it's Willow, and she's letting me do things to her I've only fantasized about. My blood is pumping hot and fast through my veins, and my dick is telling me to *move*. God, it would be so easy to reach beneath that dress and—

"Oh my God." Willow suddenly comes to her senses and backs off me, scrambling to her feet. "I'm so sorry, Reid."

"What?" Dazed, I prop myself on my elbows and shake my head. Did she just apologize?

"I'm so sorry. I should not have done that." Backed against the wall, she puts both hands over her stomach, takes a deep breath, and lets it out.

"Done what?" I'm still confused somehow.

"Kissed you."

"You didn't kiss me. I kissed you."

She shakes her head. "No, you didn't. I threw myself at you after you said you'd go to the fertility clinic with me. I just got … carried away."

"That's not how I remember it." I sit up and adjust the crotch of my pants, where my erection is bulging uncomfortably. "I made the first move."

"Did not."

"Did too."

She presses her lips together. "Jesus, Reid. Let's not fight about this. Either way, it was a mistake."

It wasn't a fucking mistake. It was everything. Mistakes are when you leave the toilet seat up and fall in later when you're half asleep. Mistakes are forgetting to lock the door or drinking too much the night before a meeting. This date tonight is a mistake.

Not kissing Willow.

"I don't think it was a mistake, Wills."

I can see the wheels turning in her head. She's trying to find a way to explain this. "Either way, this is us and we aren't this way."

"Why aren't we?"

She shakes her head and takes a step back. "Because you're Reid, and I'm ... I'm your best friend. This is crazy. It's just all this baby talk, and you're going on a date tonight, with an incredible girl ..."

The last thing I want is to go on this date. I want to pull Willow back into my arms and shut her up with my mouth. I want to strip her down, taste her, touch her, and make sense of what the hell is going on.

"That has nothing to do with what just happened here."

Willow sighs, pulling her blond hair to the side. "Please don't make more of that than it was. It was only a kiss, and it was just a heat of the moment thing. You and I ... we would never work. Let's just chalk that up to both of us being sexually frustrated."

I would love nothing more than to argue with her, but I know her—better than she knows herself some days—and she's not backing down. *Heat of the moment* would be a good explanation if I hadn't been thinking about doing that exact thing all week. And if she felt nothing, she wouldn't have kissed me back.

But Willow is an analyzer. She is going to nuke that kiss until she can't take it anymore.

"Fine," I say.

"Fine?" Her eyes widen.

"Yes, you're probably right. We have a good thing going and I wouldn't want us to fuck that up because we both just need to get laid." The next words out of my mouth will tell me everything I need to know on what she's really feeling. "It's a good thing I have a date tonight with Kandace."

Willow's eyes lock on mine. "Why is that?"

I shrug. "So I can work out all this frustration."

I watch her chest rise and fall and the heat in her eyes turn to anger. I hit a nerve. A big one.

Now I know she doesn't believe this was a random mistake.

CHAPTER EIGHT

Willow

HE KISSED ME.

Or I kissed him.

Either way, we kissed. A real kiss. Not one of those *oops I moved my head the wrong way and we pecked* kiss. No, this was a full on, oh-my-God-my-panties-just-disintegrated kiss. Reid can fucking kiss.

And after that earth-shattering kiss, I sent him on a date with Kandace, the pretty girl with blue eyes.

I hate her.

I start to pace in my apartment, cleaning up rooms that are already clean, trying not to freak the hell out. What does all of this mean anyway? We're best friends. He knows all my control issues and problems with men. He's seen me cry at movies and when I'm in my pajamas with no makeup on and day three of dry shampoo.

Reid knows all the awful crap I do, and I sure know all of his.

He's a slob who has trust issues, and he drives me crazy. He has no taste in television shows. He can barely dress himself.

He can't cook—at all. He's only ever been in one serious relationship (with Glinda the secretly wicked witch), which ended in disaster ... not that it was his fault, but still. All these things should be a red flag for me, and yet, since the other night, he's all I think about.

I'm sitting in a daze on the couch and thinking of him when a knock at the door causes me to jump.

Maybe he's back! Maybe his date was so bad that he left early and ... no, that would be bad. That would mean I failed at matchmaking—again. Dammit, I don't even know what to hope for.

I get up and look through the peephole. Aspen?

"Hey," I say as I open the door and see my sister there.

This evening, she's wearing a lovely ensemble of what looks like a burlap sack that she converted into pants and a crop top with the word MILK across the top.

She grins. "Hi, sis. I was in the neighborhood and Mom said I should stop by and see how you're doing."

"Why would she say that?"

I look across the hall, where Reid's door is, and my heart races. Behind that door, just over an hour ago, I was kissing him. Will he come by here when he's done with his date? Or is he going to take Kandace back to his place and finish what I started?

My stomach drops at the thought of that and then I want to slap myself.

Aspen stands there, looking at me. "I don't know, she just said to come by." My sister's eyes narrow. "Hmm, that's peculiar."

Great, she's getting a message from the other realm or something. "What?"

"Your aura coloring shifted from when you opened the door to just now. As soon as you looked behind me."

"My aura coloring?"

"Yes." She smiles knowingly. "Where is Reid, by the way? On his date?"

"If you must know, yes. He's on the date with Kandace—"

"The girl with crazy eyes?"

My sister is such a pain in the ass sometimes. "She's going to work out, just watch. They were both really excited about the date." I try to sound enthusiastic.

"We'll see," Aspen says, as she enters my apartment, uninvited, and plops on the couch. My phone pings. "You have a text."

I roll my eyes. "Thanks. And come on in."

Reid: At the restaurant.

I take a deep breath and reply.

Me: Have fun.
Reid: Oh, I will. Thanks for setting this up, Wills.

I hate my life.

Me: Anything for you.
Reid: Anything?
Me: Just behave and be charming.

Or don't. Ruin the date and come back. Let's cuddle up on the couch and see where the night takes us.

I'm so going to need my vibrator tonight.

"Who was that?" Aspen asks.

"Reid."

My sister smirks. "How is the lady you hope will be Mrs. Fortino?"

"He didn't say."

"Interesting." Aspen leans back, her arms draped over the back of the couch, and sighs.

I don't know why that is interesting to her, but understanding the inner workings of my sister's mind has never been my gift. Or anyone's mind. On the other hand, she's really intuitive, trustworthy, and would be able to make sense of the kiss Reid and I shared. Aspen has a weird way of seeing past the surface. She and my mother share that gift—I do not.

I wander over to the couch. "Can I ask you something?"

"Of course."

"Say … you're friends with a guy, right? And you guys have this really awesome relationship. Almost like, you just *get* each other. There's no pretense or expectation, you can just be who you are."

She nods.

"What if things … started to … change?"

"Change how?"

"Just … what if things suddenly felt different? I don't know, this is stupid." I stop myself. I'm being dumb. I already know what it means.

It means nothing.

It means that I'm horny and need to get laid.

It means that my friend and I are comfortable around each other, so it only makes sense I'd feel something when we kissed. Besides, it's been years and I've never had this issue before. Maybe it's all the talk of a baby? That would make perfect sense.

I'm anxious to have a kid and settle into the next phase of my life, and for most women, a man would be the obvious need to complete the picture. So, Reid is the man I'm with the most, therefore my subconscious has chosen him.

Voilà.

Problem solved.

"You have feelings for Reid," Aspen says with a knowing grin.

My face gets hot. "No, I don't. Not *those* feelings."

"Oh, you liar! I knew it! I knew something was different. Your eyes got all glossy when you were staring at his door." She walks over, placing her hand on my shoulder and closes her eyes. "And you guys did something!"

How in the hell does she know that? Seriously, I'm not sure if I should even move because she seems so entranced.

"Aspen," I whine softly and she opens her eyes.

"We have to go," she announces.

"Go?"

"Yes, get dressed, something covert."

"Covert?" Now I'm really confused. I grab her arm to stop her. "Aspen, please explain."

"We don't have time. Get dressed and be back out in five minutes." She turns me, slaps me on my butt, and sends me away. "Wear something that won't stand out."

Something that won't stand out? As opposed to her burlap MILK getup?

I have no idea where she thinks we need to go, but I'm terrified.

>—♡→

Thirty minutes later we are in the back of a cab heading for Randolph Street. I must be crazy.

"You're sure they're at The Darling?" Aspen asks.

"Positive. I made the reservation." I put one hand over my stomach. It won't stop jumping. "But *we're* not going to be able to get in without one."

"Just leave that to me and stay quiet."

We exit the cab and walk down the block toward the bar, our heels clicking on the sidewalk. Since I assume there's a dress code at The Darling, I made her change at my place, and after looking at photos of the bar's interior online, we decided on shades of dark brown and deep red. Our goal is to blend in. Go undercover. Spy on Reid and his date.

Okay, stalk them.

But I have myself nearly convinced I'm doing it for research purposes—just to make sure things are going okay with my project. Reid really cannot be trusted not to mess this up.

My heart races as we enter the warm, dimly lit interior, and my eyes struggle for a moment to adjust to the dark. Red leather banquettes. Velvet upholstery and drapes. Crystal chandeliers. It's sexy and romantic, the perfect place for an intimate first date. I scan the room for Reid and Kandace but don't see them.

"Good evening. Do you have a reservation?" asks the hostess, a pretty twenty-something with long dark hair and a nose ring.

"We were supposed to," says Aspen, who sounds as if she's choking up, "but I just plain forgot. It's a last minute trip, you see, and we're trying to fit everything in." She lowers her voice to a stage whisper. "My sister's only got a couple months to live."

The girl gasps. "Oh, no."

"Yes." Aspen nods sadly while I try to disappear into the woodwork. "Look at her face. That ashen color—it's terrible. And those bags under her eyes. She used to be so pretty."

"I'm very sorry," the hostess says solemnly.

"Thank you." Aspen puts a hand over her heart. "It's been so hard. Do you think you might find some little spot for us to have one little celebration of life drink? It's my birthday, and all I want is to see my sister happy one last time."

"Of course." The girl touches Aspen's shoulder. "Give me one moment."

"Thank you. Oh, and if you've got something in a corner somewhere, you know, just out of the way, that's even better. My sister doesn't like people seeing her face in this condition."

The hostess nods, her eyes wide with sympathy. "I understand completely. Let me see what I can do." She hurries away, and I smack Aspen's arm.

"Are you nuts?"

She shrugs. "What?"

"You told her I was dying!"

"No, I didn't. I only implied it, and anyway, it could be true—we don't know when our number is going to be up, Willow. Death is a part of life. No one can escape it."

I roll my eyes. "I can't believe she fell for it. And what was all that B.S. about my face?"

"I was serious about your face. And this lighting really isn't doing you any favors."

I want to hit her again, but the hostess is returning, her expression happy. "I found a cozy little nook for you. Right this way."

We follow her from the front of the bar to the back, and I keep my eyes on the feet of the patrons seated at the bar, letting my hair hang in my face so Reid won't easily spot me. I look carefully, but I don't see any shoes I recognize as his.

The "cozy little nook" turns out to be two wooden chairs along the wall between a giant potted fern and the bathroom doors.

"This is perfect," says Aspen, taking a seat in the chair next to the fern.

I take the one next to her and smile at the hostess as she hands me a menu. "Thank you."

"You're very welcome." Her face falls. "I'm so sorry about your illness, and I hope you find peace at the end of your journey."

I drop my eyes to the floor and pray I won't start to laugh. Aspen elbows me a moment later. "She's gone. Did you see them?"

"No. Did you?"

"Yeah. On that navy velvet sofa just on the other side of this plant." She gestures toward the fern. "In fact, if we're really quiet, I bet we could hear them!"

I tug her arm. "Switch places with me. I need to see better."

Aspen sighs heavily but gets up, and we swap chairs. Parting some of the fern stems with my hands, I stick my nose in the plant and peer through it. Sure enough, I can vaguely make out Reid on the far side of the sofa, facing me, and I see the back of Kandace's wavy, golden hair, which she's tossing over one shoulder as she laughs.

"Oh my God, that's so funny. You're so right!" Kandace enthuses.

Right about what? I wonder. And does she have to sit so close to him? She's sort of perched on one hip, with one elbow on the back of the sofa and her legs crossed in his direction. She's wearing a short skirt and heels. Reid is a leg man, and he has to be turned on with Kandace's long, bare limbs on display like that.

Jealousy pinches me hard, and I try to ignore it.

"What are they talking about?" Aspen whispers, hovering close behind me.

I wave a hand over my shoulder to shut her up. "I don't know yet." Turning my head so my ear is cocked toward them, I close my eyes and listen more carefully.

"My younger brother actually works there," Reid is saying. "Talk about dream job."

"Totally!" Kandace agrees.

"He comes home and talks about how hard his day at work was, and I'm like, 'Really, bro? Tough day at the comic store?'"

Kandace's squeaky giggle floats through the fern, and I wince. "Strike one, annoying laugh," I whisper to Aspen. "Sounds like nails on a chalkboard."

A server comes by, and we both order a martini, vodka for me, gin for Aspen—but only after she inquires about the botanicals in the spirit and whether it was handcrafted locally or not.

"Now what are they talking about?" Aspen pesters.

"Boring stuff. Their jobs. Colleges. Comics."

My sister frowns. "That *is* boring. Maybe they don't have any chemistry."

I perk up. "Maybe they don't."

Our drinks arrive, and I take a sip, cheerful at the thought that maybe I was wrong and Reid and Kandace aren't a good match.

And then.

"You know, this is so nice," I hear Kandace tell him. "I was really nervous about tonight because I don't really date much. My sister made me try My Heart's Desire after my last relationship ended badly, and at first, I was totally against the idea. I didn't think there was any way it would work."

"No?"

"No. I was convinced I'd be forced to go on a bunch of really terrible blind dates with slobs or jerks or creeps. But I'm happy to say I was wrong. You're none of those things."

"Are you sure?" Reid jokes.

Squeaky laugh. "Pretty sure. And you're so easy to talk to. I haven't felt so relaxed on a date in forever. So if it's all an act, don't even tell me. I don't want to know."

Reid chuckles. "Okay, I won't."

"So what about you? Have you been on many dates with the agency?"

"Never. This is my first one."

"Really?" Kandace sounds happy about that.

"Really."

"Actually, that doesn't surprise me. A guy like you probably doesn't need an agency. You must have beautiful women falling all over you all the time."

"Nah," says Reid. "Just once or twice a day."

More squeaky laughter. He's got to be annoyed by now. God knows I am.

"Handsome and funny," Kandace says. "I don't get why you're still single if you don't want to be."

"I don't mind being single," Reid tells her. "It's better than going on a lot of bad dates."

"Tell me about it. I'd pretty much given up before Willow called me with your profile as a match. She's really good at her job, isn't she?"

Aspen pokes me. "Now what are they saying?"

"Shhh," I admonish. "They're talking about me." Aspen leans over so she can hear too, practically pushing me into the plant. Her craft gin with eight botanicals spills onto my leg.

"She's pretty good at everything," Reid says, making my pulse quicken. I bring my glass to my lips for a sip and remember his tongue slipping between them earlier tonight. My stomach flips wildly.

"Oh really? Are you two friends?"

"Yeah. She lives across the hall from me."

"How nice," Kandace says in a voice that tells me she does not really think it's nice at all.

"For me, it is. Willow is the best cook in the world. I'd probably starve to death if it wasn't for her."

Kandace laughs politely but there's not much squeak to it. She leans over to the table and picks up her glass of white wine for a long swallow.

Reid, meanwhile, keeps talking about me. "She makes this Doritos casserole that's so good," he tells her.

"I don't really like Doritos," Kandace says.

Strike two, I think.

"She makes other stuff, too. Chicken parm, chili, baked ziti, this eggplant dish that I didn't think I would like but she forced me to try."

"Wow. Sounds like you two are pretty close." Kandace sets her wine glass down and shifts her position, moving a little closer to Reid.

"We are."

"Is it romantic between you?"

Reid doesn't answer right away, and I realize I won't be able to breathe until he does. I don't even know how I want him to answer, but somehow everything between us is hanging in the balance with her question. Aspen must know this, because she grabs my arm and squeezes tight.

"No," he finally replies. "It isn't."

The weight of it crushes me for no good reason. After all, it's the truth. It's *not* romantic between us. That kiss today was a mistake. That little wrestling match on my floor last week was a near miss. I shouldn't be upset about this.

Aspen sighs and sits back in her chair, sipping her drink, but I'm still paralyzed.

"Good," Kandace is saying, and now she's reaching over and touching his leg. "I don't want to get in the way if something is going on with you guys, but I'm having a really nice time. I hope you are too."

"Sure," he says without much oomph. "This is great."

"And not awkward at all," she goes on. Then she pauses. "Of course, it could get awkward later, if you're wondering whether you should kiss me goodnight."

Silence. I lean farther into the plant, pushing leaves aside so I can see Reid's expression.

He looks slightly taken aback but recovers quickly, one brow cocked up. "Yeah, I guess it could." After a sip of his drink, which looks like maybe an old fashioned, he asks, "So what's the verdict? Should I?"

A loud noise escapes me, a sort of frightened shriek. It's so loud that Aspen claps a hand over my mouth from behind.

"Definitely." Kandace's squeaky laugh is back, and she

sways toward him. "But why wait? Why not get it out of the way right now?"

I want to hit her. Seething, I lean even deeper into the plant for a better view.

How could I have thought this was a good idea?

CHAPTER NINE

Reid

THE WOMAN LEANING TOWARD ME WITH HER HAND ON my leg and her eyes on my mouth is cute, engaging, and sweet.

But she's not Willow, and I don't want to kiss her.

However, it would serve Willow right if I did kiss Kandace, considering that she is spying on us from the other side of that giant plant. Did she think I wouldn't notice her and Aspen sneaking in and staking out right behind us? It's fucking ridiculous how obvious they are.

But right now, I've got a bigger problem.

"I'm a man who likes the element of surprise," I tell Kandace. "I think it's more romantic."

Her face falls, but she smiles as she sits back. "You're right. A surprise kiss *is* more romantic."

And it's right at that moment that Willow topples off her chair and into the plant before landing on the floor on her back, her martini glass clattering on the dark wood.

Kandace squeals, clapping a hand over her heart. "Oh my

goodness, are you okay?"

Willow looks a little stunned but grabs her glass, pops to her feet, and smooths her hair. "I'm fine."

"Aren't you … Willow? From the agency?" Kandace asks in confusion.

"Yes. Hello." She plasters a smile on her face and looks from Kandace to me. "Fancy seeing you here. What a coincidence."

I cross my arms over my chest and decide to mess with her. "Not really, since *you* made the reservation for us."

She blinks at me several times, probably wishing her glass wasn't empty and she had something to toss in my face. "Did I? I must have forgotten."

"Must have." I give her a grin.

"Well, we should be going, Aspen," Willow says to her sister. "We're scouting out several different places tonight to send potential matches," she tells us, as if that explains what she was doing hiding in a plant. "Enjoy your evening."

"You too," Kandace says as Willow grabs her sister by the sleeve and drags her to the front of the bar. "That was odd, wasn't it?" she asks once we're alone.

"Not if you know those two. Wills is usually pretty sane, but her sister is certifiable."

"You're … close with her family?" Kandace picks up her wine again.

"I don't know if I'd say close, but I've known them for years. They're a little nutty, but they're good people."

Kandace switches the subject then, and we order another round of drinks. The next hour I spend with her is perfectly pleasant, so I ask her to dinner, mostly because I'm starving at that point.

We enjoy a leisurely meal and expensive bottle of wine at a nice Italian restaurant, and she's all the things Willow promised she would be, but I don't feel any spark. So after paying the bill, I walk her out, give her a hug and friendly kiss on the cheek, and put her in a cab. I can tell from the look on her face she's disappointed, but what was I supposed to do? Pretend to be more interested than I was? Waste her time? Take her home and bang her just to get rid of the tension?

I wouldn't do that—although believe me, I thought about it for a hot second.

But she's not Willow. And Willow is all I can think about.

I walk back to our apartment building in no particular hurry, trying to work out in my head what's going on in my heart. Or at least in my pants.

I've always found Willow attractive, but it's never been worth wrecking what has come to be the closest relationship I've ever had with anyone, male or female, outside of my brother. Willow knows me. She gets me. And she still loves me. I don't want to fuck with that, so I understand why she called that kiss a mistake. If I give in to whatever is pulling me toward her, I worry that I'll lose the one person in my world who sees me for who I am and accepts me, faults and all.

Because what the fuck do I know about how to make a woman happy?

I cross the street, hands in my pockets. I certainly never saw an example growing up with my parents. I thought I made Glinda happy, and look what happened. She said I was a terrible boyfriend who took her for granted. She called me selfish and immature. She told me I never really let her in, and maybe she was right. Maybe I hadn't. Maybe deep down, some part of me knew I shouldn't trust her.

Still, the breakup sucked and I never want to go through that shit again.

But what am I going to do about these crazy feelings for Willow? They don't feel like the same old urges to get her naked. They're stronger and more intense. They can't be buried or shoved aside. They're like this constant pressure inside me, these nagging questions that refuse to leave me alone.

What would it be like to have her that way? Skin to skin? Breathless and begging? My body inside hers?

I want answers, I think as I open the door to our building.

No, I *need* them.

I take the elevator up to our floor and go right to her apartment. Using the key she gave me, I unlock her door, smiling that she still hasn't changed the lock, and head inside.

"Reid?" She jumps off the couch and I freeze.

Jesus, she's fucking beautiful. I've seen her a million times like this, but I don't know what it is—I can't breathe.

Her hair is piled up on top of her head in some sort of nest, the glasses that she swears she doesn't need are on, and her legs … God, her legs. Long, sweet, slender … they would look perfect around my neck.

"What are you doing here? If this is about …" She stops talking and looks at me, her eyes full of confusion as I watch her chest rise and fall.

I walk toward her, unable to stand still. My hands grip her cheeks, and I pull her mouth to mine. Her gasp is swallowed by the searing kiss. Her fingers wrap around my wrists and I don't know if she's trying to stop me, but I'm going to keep going until she does.

Yet she never does. Instead of pushing me away, her hands move to my hips.

Willow kisses me back.

She kisses me like this is the only option.

She kisses me harder and more passionately than the last time.

She gives as much as she takes and I fucking revel in it.

This is crazy, but I don't care. It's right. It's everything that finally makes sense. I wondered what it would be like and now I know—it's fucking perfect.

"Reid." She says my name and then pulls my mouth back to hers.

I kiss her, loving how our mouths fit and the way her tongue feels against mine.

"Tell me to stop." I give her an out that I pray she won't take.

"What?"

"Tell me now, Wills."

I'm desperate for her. Seeing her tonight, knowing she was spying on me, did something to my heart that I can't explain. It was the answer to the question that neither of us was willing to face.

There's something here.

Maybe it's new. Maybe it's always been there but we didn't see it. Maybe Willow and I needed to be pushed. Whatever the reason, the outcome is this.

She touches my face. Her fingertips are soft, and she moves her thumb to my lip. "I can't. I don't know what's happening, but I don't want it to stop."

"Good, because I don't think I could."

My mouth is back to hers the second the words are out.

She giggles against my lips and I drink it in. Everything about Willow is sweet. Her mouth, her laughter, her heart. They all make her irresistible. I don't know how I never saw it.

I break the kiss and scoop her into my arms, bringing her back to the bedroom. She doesn't say anything, and I'm glad for it.

We're both always in our heads and I'm very much ready to be in her instead.

I lay her down and crawl over her, loving how she looks at me with lust-filled eyes. "Tell me what you want, Wills." She shakes her head and I know what she's doing, but I'm not having it. "Don't think, baby, just tell me."

Her lids fall, closing me off to what she doesn't want me to see, and I take a beat to really look at her. Lips swollen, shirt falling off her shoulder, hair fanning out on the bed. She looks like an angel.

"I want you to kiss me," she whispers.

I do as she asks, leaning down, kissing her for just long enough and then pull back. "Like that?"

She nods. "More."

"More? How much more?"

Willow wraps her hand around my neck, this time not willing to speak, but willing to show me. I fucking love it. I love when a woman is confident in bed and will take what she wants. I moan into her mouth and then she pushes me back.

"What do you want, Reid?"

"You, this, everything."

She grins. "Be more specific."

Who am I to deny the lady? "Sit up."

I watch as she leans up and then grabs the bottom of her shirt, lifting it over her head. She's not wearing a bra, and I thank God for small miracles.

My hands are on her breasts, kneading and squeezing, watching how she responds. I've thought about this in so many ways, but actually feeling her skin is something else.

She's something else.

In some ways, I think that Willow and I always knew this would happen. They say guys and girls can't be just friends, but we were—until we weren't. I don't know when it changed, but I thank the Lord that it did.

"Fuck, Wills," I say and then press my lips to hers.

Her hands are on my shirt, lifting it up. We break apart just long enough to remove it, and then I need to kiss her again. I'm kissing her for all the times that I could have and didn't. I'm kissing her because if she fucking stops to think and goes back in her head, she'll push me away, and I want all I can get.

"Reid, please," she whimpers and I could blow my load right now.

Hearing her say my name like that is almost too much.

"What do you want, sweetheart?"

"Touch me."

My hands are on her breasts already, so I know it's not that. "It would be my pleasure."

I slide my palms down her perfect body, loving how she squirms beneath me. I reach for her shorts and pull them off.

I take a second, because this is Willow. My Willow. And she's naked.

"You have no idea how beautiful you are, Wills."

Her cheeks flame and I see a hint of her retreat. Hell no. I need to touch her, taste her, feel her, so I move in.

She didn't say how she wanted me to touch her, so I take the liberty of deciding for her.

My tongue slides around her nipple, teasing, nipping just enough to make her stop thinking, and my hand slips between us. I find her clit and rub circles while mimicking the motion with my tongue.

Willow moans, her head tossing from side to side. Her breathing grows louder and more rapid as I make her climb.

I want to make her come so many times she can't see straight. The male ego inside of me is roaring to make her forget every other man and desire no one but me.

As she starts to move her legs, I know she's getting close and I have to taste her.

"Reid!" she calls out when I remove my hand, and I don't waste a second.

I grip her legs, tossing them over my shoulder, and then I run my tongue against her pussy. She lets out a loud groan and I do it again.

Her hands grip my hair, both pushing me away and then holding me close. I take my time, making her sweat it out, make her work for her release. Sure, I could make it easier on her, but my entire goal is to drag this out as long as I can. I need her desperate for it.

"Jesus. Please. Reid ... I'm so ... so close!"

I increase the pressure from my tongue, and start to finger her at the same time, wishing it was my dick inside her. She's soft, warm, and if I don't get my cock inside her, I might possibly die.

Seriously. It could happen.

"Let go, Willow," I say and then gently use my teeth on her clit.

She's fighting it, barely holding on, until she can't anymore. She calls out my name as she finally finds the edge, her breathing is labored, and I could listen to her say it that way a million times.

I climb up her body, her hands pressing against my chest. "That was ..." But I can't even describe it.

"Yeah."

"I want you, Wills. Now."

She nods. "I want you too."

I push up, looking down at the girl who has turned my entire world upside down in only a week.

Her hands lift to my pants, removing my belt, then undoing the button, and I push them down, letting my rock-hard dick spring free.

Willow and I have technically seen each other naked, but this is like looking at each other for the first time.

She smirks, and I swear I get even harder. There's something sexy about a woman looking at your cock and smiling.

I lean over into her top drawer where I know she keeps condoms and the vibrator she claims she doesn't have. I grab one of the packets and tear it open.

"Reid?" Her voice is filled with fear.

Dear God, please don't want to stop.

"What's wrong?"

"Nothing, it's just … I don't want this to change us."

"I thought you wanted things to change."

"Not like this. I mean, this is … we need to …" She lets out a heavy sigh. "You're my best friend and this can't change that, okay?"

"Nothing will change. I'm not going anywhere. Do you want me to stop?"

She shakes her head. "No."

"Good."

I line myself up and try to think of anything to keep from embarrassing myself. I go over financials in my mind while I slide in.

Four hundred emails to answer.

Holy fucking shit she's tight.

Two meetings next week.

Dear God, I might explode.

I inch a little farther.

There are about seven ad accounts that need to be re-looked at.

"Reid. Please!"

And then, Willow grips my ass, pulling me as deep as I can get, and I don't remember a fucking thing after that.

CHAPTER TEN

Willow

I HAD SEX WITH REID.

Really, really good sex.

Of course he couldn't suck in bed and make it easier on me. Nope. He had to be fantastic and give me multiples.

Multiples! Like a damn unicorn walked up to me and tapped me on the nose!

Now he's in my bed, snoring with his arm draped over me, and I can't sleep.

I told him everything was fine. I did the whole *let's cuddle* thing because he looked so happy. I can't remember the last time I saw him smile like that. I'm a fool, that's for damn sure.

And he thinks nothing will change? Was he kidding? *Everything* has changed. We had sex, and I'm ruined for all men now.

I have to think. I need to figure out what the hell all of this means and how I'm going to fix it.

Because it has to be fixed. Reid and I aren't like that. We aren't a couple. We aren't in love. We're just two best friends who got a little carried away and gave in to an itch that has needed to be scratched for a while now.

Yes, that's it. Curiosity, plus a natural, biological attraction and a dash of loneliness. Add that all together and you have a recipe for a one-night stand that was really great and all, thanks to Reid's unicorn dick, but we can't let it happen again. It isn't worth ruining our friendship.

I know I said I wanted things to change, but I didn't mean us. Not like this.

I have no idea what time it is, but the sun is coming up and my room is starting to glow with morning light. I scoot my legs over the side of the bed, making sure not to wake him, while trying to lift his arm up just enough to get out. When my feet hit the floor, I slide a little more, moving when I can. Reid makes a loud sound and I'm half on and half off the bed, hoping I can slip out entirely.

He lets out a loud snore that sounds more like a roar, and I use the opportunity to go.

Of course, I didn't account for my rug sliding out from under my foot, and I tumble to the floor with a loud bang.

"Ouch!" I grab my left elbow and rub it.

"Willow?" Reid peeks over the edge of the bed at me. His hair is sticking up in all directions and his jaw is stubbled, but still my heart beats faster. "What are you doing? Running away?"

"Uh, no. I was just trying to get out of bed without waking you." Suddenly I remember how naked I am. Scrambling to my feet, I hurry over to my dresser and grab a T-shirt. As I throw it over my head, I will my pulse to stop racing.

"You've got a cute butt."

I meet his eyes in the mirror. "Thanks."

"Come back to bed and let me get my hands on it again."

Part of me wants to take a running leap onto the mattress and let him do that and more, but I know I can't. "I don't think so."

"Why not?"

I turn around and face him, leaning back against the dresser. "Because we can't do that again."

"Sure, we can. We can do it right this very minute."

"No, Reid." I fold my arms across my chest. "I have to take a shower and get ready for work, and you have to go back to your apartment now."

Reid sits up and scratches his head. The blankets fall to his waist, and I'm forced to contemplate his smooth, muscular chest. I can still feel the weight of it on mine, still smell his warm, bare skin, still remember the way his arms had been braced above my shoulders. "Why are you upset about this?" he asks.

"I'm not upset. I'm just facing reality. You and I are not a thing, we're never going to be a thing, so we shouldn't go through the motions of a thing, because it's confusing." I speak firmly and with finality, praying he's not going to push back.

"I'm not confused." He looks me right in the eye. "I know what I feel."

"Well, I'm confused. And I don't think you actually know how you feel, I think you're just reacting to the sex. Sex can make you believe you feel things for another person, when really it's just the chemicals in your body. The oxytocin and whatnot. It isn't real."

Reid keeps staring at me, and for a moment I'm worried that he knows me too well, and he's going to call me on my bullshit. But he doesn't.

"Okay, Willow. If that's what you think."

"It is," I confirm, relief coursing through me as he starts looking around for his clothing. "And I'm positive you'll think the same as soon as you get a little perspective."

"Right." Spotting his boxer briefs on the floor near the bed, he tosses the blankets aside and swings his feet to the floor.

Quickly, I turn around and start pulling things from my dresser drawers—underwear, a bra, a pair of dark skinny jeans. I don't want to see his naked body. It will only mess me up more, and my emotions are already wreaking havoc in my belly. "I'm going to jump in the shower. Can you let yourself out?"

"Yep."

Behind me I hear the metallic clink of a belt buckle. The hum of a zipper. "Great. I'll catch up with you later."

"Whatever."

I avoid looking at him as I make my way into the bathroom. Once I've made it to safety, I shut the door, lock it, and lean back against it. Fighting the fierce urge to cry, I close my eyes and hold my breath.

Please leave, Reid. I can't handle talking about this right now. I can't deal with your disappointed face or your naked body or your feelings. Please understand, you're the best friend I've ever had, and I don't want to lose that. I need you on my side for the rest of my life, and if I open myself up to you, and you decide I'm not what you want, I'll never recover. It's not worth the risk.

I stay there choking back sobs until I hear the door to my apartment slam shut. Then I turn on the water, slip my shirt over my head, and step under the spray, finally letting the tears fall.

"Uh oh. What happened to you?" Aspen asks the moment she sees me at my desk that morning. Coming closer, she frowns at me and waves both hands in front of my face in a wax-on, wax-off motion. "Your aura is all kinds of fucked up."

I push her hands away. "Leave my aura alone today. Okay?"

"No can do, sis. When I sense a tortured soul in need of unburdening itself, I'm compelled to help it along. It's part of my gift." She drops onto the floor and sits in a lotus position. "Talk to me."

Heaving a sigh, I close my laptop and rub my face with both hands. "I did something stupid."

"Like what?"

I peek at her between my fingers. "I slept with Reid."

She nods thoughtfully. "Of course you did. I could sense the anticipatory sexual tension between the two of you last night, and the five brightest planets in the sky were aligned and visible, including Venus and Mars, and we all know what that means."

I have no idea what that means, but maybe I can blame astronomy for what happened last night. "It was the craziest thing. I came home after we left them at the bar. I ate dinner. I put on my pajamas and watched the Hallmark channel, and I was just about to go to bed when Reid came bursting into my apartment, breathing hard and chest all puffed up like he was furious with me."

Aspen sighs. "Fucking Mars. Every time."

"I thought he was mad about us spying on him and Kandace and I tried to apologize, but out of nowhere he just grabs me and kisses me so hard I can't breathe." I shake my head, remembering the shock of his lips on mine. "I tried to fight him off, because I knew it was a terrible idea, but instead of pushing him away, I suddenly found myself kissing him back."

"That's Venus for you," my sister says with a sly smile.

"Then before I knew it, he was sweeping me off my feet and rushing into my bedroom, where we proceeded to throw all rational thought out the window and bang each other senseless."

"How was it?" Aspen's grin is sly.

Sighing, I set my elbows on my desk and tip my forehead onto my fingers. "Amazing. Magical. Perfection."

"So he knows what he's doing?"

I nod miserably. "And then some."

"Was it awkward afterward?"

"It was, and it wasn't." I sit back in my chair. "Right afterward, we fell asleep pretty quickly. But at some point, I woke up and started to panic."

"Why?"

"Because I realized what a mistake we made!" Hopping to my feet, I grab my empty coffee cup and stalk over to the Keurig I keep on top of my credenza. "I was lying there, naked, next to Reid, and we'd done all the things!" Flustered, I shove a pod in the machine and snap it shut.

"Good grief, Willow, you had sex with him, that's all. It's a totally natural, human thing to do. The world didn't explode, no one was hurt, and orgasms are good for you. What is there to panic about?"

While my coffee cup fills, I think about all the answers I could give, all the frightening things running through my head all night, keeping me awake. There are almost too many to name, but will Aspen understand any of them? She believes in free love and no rules and following your heart's desire. But I don't trust my heart to lead me in the right direction right now.

"It comes down to this," I say, carefully carrying my coffee back to my desk. "Reid's friendship is more important to me than anything, even good sex. I'm willing to sacrifice good sex in order to preserve the dynamic we have right now. I need him in my life, Aspen. And if we let our sexual attraction take over our decision-making, we're just asking for trouble. I know it."

"How do you know?"

"Because it felt too good," I blurt, coffee sloshing over the side of my cup as I set it down. "It was too intense and too much fun and too hot. That kind of fire dies out fast. It doesn't last. And I'd rather be celibate than lose Reid."

My sister exhales as if I'm a hopeless case. "Okay, fine. But remember." She draws herself up and lays the back of her hands on her legs, palms up. "Fear does not stop death. It stops life."

I cock my head. "Where did you hear that? Your last fortune cookie?"

"No. I found it on Pinterest. There's some really good stuff there."

Dropping into my chair, I roll my eyes. "Thanks for the tip. Now I have work to do, so please find someone else's soul to unburden."

"Fine." She unfolds her legs, stands up, and heads for the door. When she gets there, she looks over her shoulder at me. "So are you still planning to match him up with someone?"

The thought turns my stomach. "Yes. That's my job."

"And he agrees with you about last night being a mistake?"

"Yes," I lie.

Aspen gives me a look that clearly expresses her disapproval and disappears down the hall.

It doesn't matter what she thinks, I tell myself. It only matters what Reid and I think, and I'm certain that once he takes a moment to consider the potential fallout, he'll agree. After all, he was the one who said he didn't want anything to change.

We shouldn't have done it, and we can't do it again.

There's too much at stake.

CHAPTER ELEVEN

Reid

I SHOULD HAVE KNOWN SHE WAS GOING TO FREAK OUT.

Actually, I did know. It's totally Willow. And even knowing that, I would have gone there last night. I was too fed up with wondering what it would be like.

Now I know.

Unfortunately, I'm not sure if that makes it better or worse, since what I know is that she and I are fucking fantastic together. Not just the physical stuff, which was beyond even my wildest dreams—and my dreams about her have gotten pretty wild—but how much fun we had. How much we laughed. How good it felt to know it was Willow inviting me inside her. How unreal it felt to have her hands on my skin and her breath on my lips and her voice in my ear, panting *yes, yes, yes*. That girl can be the most uptight, persnickety little thing on the planet, day to day, but in bed she was all liquid fire.

And I made her come at least twice. I know I did.

So what's her problem? I tighten the knot in my tie and study my reflection in the full-length mirror in my bedroom, trying to figure this out. Why was she in such a hurry to kick me out of her bed this morning?

Across the hall, she's getting ready for work too, and I imagine her fretting about what we've done and coming up with a million reasons why it was a mistake. Each one would be sensible, logical, and irrefutable.

My stupid gut feeling we could be great together wouldn't stand a chance.

But fuck that. I've got to give it one.

As I'm leaving my room, I run into Leo attempting to enter it.

"Dude, I didn't think you were here," he says, scratching his stomach. He's wearing ripped boxer shorts and a white Superman T-shirt with yellowed armpits.

I frown. "I didn't sleep here, but I came in this morning to get ready for work. Do you need something?"

"Coming to use your bathroom. It's a lot cleaner than mine."

"Jesus Christ, Leo. It's called Lysol. Go buy some. I gave you a place to stay, but I'm not scrubbing your fucking toilet."

My brother looks taken aback. "Did you wake up on the wrong side of the bed or something? What's with the bad mood?"

"I'm not in a bad mood!" I roar. "And I don't need to be told by you or Willow or anybody else how I feel!"

Leo nods knowingly. "Ah. I get it. You slept with Willow."

I stare at him. "How do you know that?"

He taps his head. "I'm smart. And I notice things, like the way you look at her. It's the same way I looked at the June 1938 Action Comics book No. 1. I saw it once at a show. A real beauty." He sighs. "But way out of my price range."

"Yeah, well, you have a better chance of buying that comic book than I do of convincing Willow to give me a chance."

"I don't think so. That thing costs millions of dollars." He burps and scratches his belly again. "Anyway, what's with Willow? Why won't she give you a chance?"

"Hell if I know."

"Maybe you're a shitty lay."

I glare at him. "Fuck off."

"I'm serious. Are you sure you did it right? Do you need some tips on how to find her—"

I hold out a hand to shut him up. "I don't need any sex tips, thank you very much. I know where everything is. Our problem isn't physical, it's mental. She thinks sleeping together was a mistake."

"Oh." Leo actually looks a little sad for me. "So now what do you do?"

"I convince her otherwise." I stand up taller. "She's just scared is all. And I get it—we've been best friends for years, and we don't want to lose that."

"You can't push her, though. Willow is stubborn."

"I know that," I snap, annoyed that Leo, of all people, is trying to give me dating advice. "I know her better than anyone."

"I'm just saying, you might want to keep that Italian temper of yours in check and not go charging at her like a bull toward a red cape."

"I know what I'm doing," I insist, pushing past him.

But it's not exactly true.

I text her around one that afternoon.

> Me: Drink after work? My treat.
> Willow: I'm meeting friends for dinner.

Is she really? Or is it an excuse not to see me because she's worried I'm going to try to sleep with her again? I tell a fib to get her to meet with me.

> Me: I've got dinner plans too. We can make it quick.
> Willow: Oh, okay then. Where?
> Me: The Kerryman? Six?
> Willow: Sounds good.

I set my phone aside and concentrate on work for the rest of the day, but she's on my mind a lot. If I close my eyes, I see her beneath me. Then I inhale, and I swear I can still smell her. I get caught doing that once, by my secretary.

"Everything okay?" she asks from the doorway of my office.

My eyes fly open and I cough. "Yes. Just ... thinking deep thoughts." Deep, penetrative thoughts.

"Okay," she says, giving me a strange look.

At twenty to six, I leave work and walk over to the Kerryman, again feeling like the cool air will do me good. Every time I think of her, I get all hot beneath my clothes. And even though I snapped at my brother this morning, deep down I know he's not wrong—I do have a temper, and it gets the better of me sometimes. I tend to let my emotions run roughshod over my rational thoughts. So a few deep breaths of crisp autumn air might be helpful.

When I arrive, she's already there, sitting at the busy bar and nursing a glass of whiskey on the rocks. There are no empty seats near her.

"Hey," I say, putting my hand on her shoulder.

"Hey." She turns and looks at me. Her smile seems tentative. "Sorry there isn't another stool."

"No problem. I can stand." The bartender comes by, and I order a pint of Guinness. "How was your day?"

"Good." She nods a little too enthusiastically. "Yours?"

"Good." My beer arrives, and both of us take a sip of our drinks. "I was thinking we could talk about what happened last night ... and this morning."

"I don't want to talk about it," she says quickly, dropping her eyes to the bar. "We need to forget it happened."

"Hey. Look at me."

When she doesn't, I set down my beer and take her chin in my hand, forcing her to meet my eyes. "I will never forget last night, not in a million fucking years. It meant everything to me."

"Reid, stop," she whispers.

The rest of the room fades away. I'm standing close enough to smell her perfume. Our lips are only inches apart. Her eyes are saying things her mouth won't.

God, I want to kiss her.

I want to feel her against me, hear her moans, drown in her eyes again as she watches me fuck her brains out.

What would she do if I crushed my lips to hers right now? If I took away her ability to argue with me? If I showed her, right here in this bar, with everybody watching, how much I want her?

I lean toward her, but she pushes me away.

"Don't," she says, her eyes filling with tears. "I can't handle it."

"Can't handle what?" I demand, grabbing my beer for a long pull.

Trying to compose herself, she runs her fingers through her long blond hair. "You're too important to me, Reid. This friendship matters too much, and then there's the fact that my job is kind of on the line."

My head jerks back and I take a step back. "Your job?"

What does her job have to do with this?

"Yes. We need to find you a match so that I can prove to my mother I'm ready to take over the company. You're not going to back out, are you?"

I can't believe she actually thinks I want to go on another one of these dates after last night. For someone who knows me, right now she's freaking clueless.

"What we did was not a mistake, and even if it was, I'd do it again," I tell her.

"Don't say that." She looks around like she's uncomfortable.

"I don't care who hears me. I want *you*, Willow. I'm not going on any more meaningless dates with girls I have zero interest in."

Her lips part and I see her trying to figure out what to say. "But ... I need you to. I need to prove to everyone that I can do this. You're not going to follow through now? Just because we had sex?"

"I'm not going to follow through because I have no interest in being matched."

"You agreed to this. You said you'd at least try and give me six months."

I know what I said, and I hate letting her down, but I don't see how she can think this is a good idea. "How the hell is that even going to work? You don't really want me to date anyone, either."

"Yes, I do! I set you up!" She puts a hand on her chest. "I'm the one who put you on that date."

The date she showed up to? Yeah, she's really selling me on this. "Do you not remember you skulking in the plants to spy on my date?"

She sniffs. "I wasn't skulking."

"No? What do you call it?"

"Supervising. I was making sure that you didn't screw it up. Which you did."

I laugh once and take another long draw of my beer. This girl is delusional. "It had nothing to do with the fact that I kissed you right before the date?"

"*I* kissed *you*."

"No, that's not what happened, but let's just pretend that your twisted version of that kiss is right ... why did you show up at my date, huh?"

We both know it had nothing to do with her supervising anything. After being in her body, I was also in her head. Just like she's been in mine every damn waking moment since the night we almost kissed on her floor.

"I already told you. I was ... overseeing things."

I cross my arms over my chest. "And I'm calling bullshit. We both know you have feelings for me."

"I do not!" She rises from her stool and straightens her back, giving me a clear shot down her blouse. What I wouldn't give to rip it off her again.

"Well, that's another thing I'm calling bullshit on."

I know I'm pushing her way too hard, but she's driving me crazy. It's one thing to deny she wants me like I know she does, but to try to set me up with someone else? It's fucking sadistic!

"I *don't* have feelings for you," she snaps. "Not those kinds of feelings. But I do have a dinner date with someone I'd much rather be around right now."

She tosses a twenty down on the bar and then starts to walk out.

Oh, no, we're not done here.

I throw another ten bucks down, drain my beer, and head toward the door after her. "Willow! Stop!"

She halts on the sidewalk but doesn't turn around. I move closer to her, waiting for her to look at me.

"What do you want, Reid?" There's an edge to her voice that throws me.

My chest is to her back, and I bring my hands up to her shoulders. I wish we weren't on the busy streets of Chicago. I would give anything to be in one of our apartments, where I could strip her down and feel her soft skin again. But more than anything, I need her to know how I feel—without getting angry about it.

"Why did you run away?" I ask, tempering my tone. "This morning."

She shakes her head as I close my eyes, inhaling the light scent of lavender from her shampoo. "Why does it matter?" she asks.

Because you matter to me. "I want to know."

Willow's body is tense, as though she's hanging onto the same fraying end of the rope I am. "It's not important."

"It is to me."

She turns slowly, her eyes lifting to meet mine. "We can't do this. I won't do this. You're my best friend. You and I can't date because we know exactly where it would end up. We're nothing alike! And we've got problems, Reid—I hate that you're a temperamental jackass, and you can't stand my nagging. You have commitment issues, and I want a baby. What part of that sounds like a promising start?"

I find myself unable to argue back. Nothing she said is wrong. We're not right for each other on paper. I'll be the first to admit that, but then why does my heart refuse to agree? Because while there are probably a hundred good reasons to walk away, I can't make myself do it.

I want her too much.

I want to see her all the fucking time—I wanted it even before we slept together. Can't she see how good it could be?

"Can you honestly tell me that you don't feel anything more than friendship?" I ask. "Can you look me in the eye and say that you feel nothing? Have you been able to think of anything else since that night I tackled you in your towel?"

Willow breathes in and out softly. Her lips part, but no sound comes out. I know what that means.

She doesn't want to lie to me. She feels the way I do, but she's thought about it all too much and it's freaking her out.

"That's what I thought."

"Reid, I have to go."

"In a minute." I place my hands on her shoulders again. "You said you wanted things to change. It was *me* who wanted them to stay the same."

"I don't want them to change like this." Her lower lip trembles. "There's too much at stake."

I'm so frustrated with her I could scream. I've never been

a sit-back-and-wait-it-out kind of guy, but I have a feeling that's what I'm going to need to do. Pushing Willow is only going to make her retreat further. But I can't resist moving in to press my lips to hers like I've wanted to since the minute I saw her. Only then do I pull back, letting her go. "I'll see you soon, Wills. Enjoy your dinner."

Then I walk away, hoping she's standing there, still gaping at me.

CHAPTER TWELVE

Willow

"HE KISSED YOU AGAIN?" ASPEN ASKS AS WE SIT at the table. "Jesus, what the hell is with him?" She pops another fry in her mouth while shaking her head.

"That's what I want to know!" I go to grab one as well, but my stomach does another flip, reminding me I'm too anxious to eat.

Aspen, on the other hand, has had no issues eating both her dinner and mine. Which is hilarious since this wasn't even supposed to be a real dinner. It was just me forcing my sister to meet me so I had a damn excuse to avoid him. And I figured we could spend a little time going over the other prospects we had for Reid.

I can't tell if it's the kiss or the mere thought of him dating one of these girls making me feel sick to my stomach.

Seeing him at the bar was not what I anticipated. I knew it would be awkward because all I kept picturing was him naked and on top of me. When he was standing close, I could smell his cologne, and I remembered how good it smelled mixed with his sweat. Which then took my mind to how good it felt when he touched me.

And then I was staring at him and wishing I could jump him, rip his clothes off in the bar's bathroom, turn the memory into a reality.

Aspen snaps her fingers in front of my face. "Willow? You in there?"

I drop my head on the table. "Why is he in my damn head? Why is he doing this to me?"

"Because he has feelings for you. It's clear that the planets are shifting in your favor. Once they line up, it's going to be out of your hands. The Earth and her siblings are in control."

I lift my head and glare at her. "I'm pretty sure it's all in *our* control, but whatever."

"Have you tried to prevent the gravitational pull of planets? It's not possible, so neither you nor Reid will be able to stop it. You're going to have to sit back and let this happen. Let your souls come together as two celestial bodies with an inevitable fate."

Dear God. "I'm seriously wondering if you're from this planet at all."

She shrugs. "I'm just telling you how I see it."

I need another drink. "I regret asking this already, but how exactly do you see it? Where do we end up?"

Aspen is weird, but at the same time, she's got the gift like my mother. They're much more intuitive about the concept of matchmaking. It's a gut feeling they have when a couple is together. I've always thought it was crazy, but I can't deny the results.

"You're going to marry him," she says imperiously.

I burst out laughing. "You're insane! Reid isn't going to marry anyone, ever, and I'm going to die alone, because once Mom sells the business I'll be broke and unable to afford to have a baby!"

"That may be, Willow, but you truly love him and he truly loves you. That's rare, and if he's willing to look past your bad fashion sense and weird quirks, I'd go with it."

"You think *I* have bad fashion sense? What exactly is it that you're wearing right now?" I gesture across the table at her getup.

Today, my sister is wearing a "Jesus Won't Save You" T-shirt with what appear to be plastic pants. *Plastic.* They're sort of hard looking, but shiny at the same time. I'm pretty sure she melted water bottles and then molded them. Or maybe they were garbage bags once upon a time. Either way, I'm not brave enough to touch them.

"I'm a conservationist," she says, as if that explains everything.

"Is that what we're calling it?"

Aspen rolls her eyes. "You can deflect all you want, but your stubborn denial is keeping the stars from aligning for you."

"I thought it was planets?"

"It's all part of the celestial universe, Willow," she says with an air of mystery, wiggling her fingers in the air.

This is too much. "What about reality? What about the fact that he's got a boatload of baggage and we have very different goals for the future? What about the fact that in all these years, Reid and I have never felt anything like this before?"

Aspen spins the straw in her drink. "Does any of that matter when it comes to love?"

I sigh and sit back. Why am I asking her about this? She's never even been in love. Hell, I'm not sure Aspen has dated anyone in months because it's really hard to find a man who is cool with a woman living in an Airstream without running water. "I don't love him like that."

She laughs. "Okay."

"I don't." If I keep saying it, maybe I'll believe it.

"Yep. I hear you."

"I'm serious," I say with more conviction.

"Uh huh."

"Aspen."

"Willow."

Now I remember why I hated her as a kid. "I'm not talking about this anymore."

"Okay. Then let's find his next date like you wanted us to and see if you don't lose your mind."

I grab my wine glass and drain it. "Great. Perfect. Let's work."

We open up the book, and I really want to draw mustaches and horns on each one of the girls when I think about them with Reid.

Because I don't love him like that, and I'm completely okay with him kissing them.

But I give the prettiest one a beard.

And a wart for good measure.

I sniff as I grab another tissue from the box, wiping my snot and tears. This TV show … it's killing me.

Those two characters love each other so much, and they

can't be together. Why? Because the guy is dumb, that's why.

They're all dumb.

Reid is dumb. It's been three days and he hasn't come over, called, snuck in and eaten my food—nothing.

I purposely made pot roast in the slow cooker yesterday, because I know that smell always fills the hallway. You can't avoid it, and that man's olfactory sense when it comes to food is off the charts.

I thought watching my shows would cheer me up, but instead it's slowly breaking me. Reid is breaking me. Because the truth is … I miss him.

I miss spending time with him, even when it's just watching television. I miss him complaining that my shows are too sappy. I miss him listening to me bitch about my job when my mother is being overbearing and ridiculous. I want to cook for him, see him come over and enjoy my food.

Why won't he? Can't we get past this already?

Frustrated, I sit up straight and blow my nose one last time. This is silly. He's my best friend, and whatever happened between us that night can't take that away.

I hop off the couch and head out into the hallway. I'm standing in front of his door, not sure if I should knock or just go in, when it flies open.

"Willow?" Leo asks, stumbling back a little. "Oh, hey."

"Hey, is … umm … is Reid here?"

He looks me over with a grin. "Did you forget something?"

"What?"

"Pants."

I look down and my shirt is hanging over my shorts, giving the illusion I have no pants on. Awesome.

"I have shorts on … Leo, your brother? Is he here?"

"No, he's not. He said he was going out for drinks."

"Oh." I sigh.

"He didn't tell you?"

No, he didn't tell me. But I lie to Leo. "You know, he mentioned something about it, it just slipped my mind."

Leo chuckles. "Or you both are being idiots and still not talking …"

I'm not having this conversation. Leo is the last person who should be calling anyone names. Still, I'm surprised he knows anything and now I'm intrigued.

"Did Reid say something to you?"

He shrugs. "Just that you guys slept together and now you're being weird."

I slap a hand to my chest, furious. "He said *I'm* being weird? Like he's not? He's the one who's ignoring me!"

"I agree, he's being weird too. I mean, it's like you two are basically married, but now that you've consummated it, you're not sure what to do."

"I'm sure I'd like to punch him in the throat," I fume.

He smiles, as if he'd like to see that. "So go call him, or better yet, go see him. He's at the bar next to his office. Go blow up his date."

"*Date?*" My blood boils higher.

"Oh, I didn't mention that he was having drinks with the new girl at his company?"

He's on a date. He's on a date with a girl I didn't set up. He's on a date with a girl I didn't set up after he kissed me again.

I'm going to kill him.

I don't say another word to Leo, because why bother? It'll just delay Reid's death and right now, that's my single focus.

Kiss me and then go on a date?

I head into my apartment, toss on a pair of sweatpants and a hoodie. His office is just a few blocks from here and I know exactly what bar he's at. Of course, it's pouring rain, but I barely feel it. I'm so mad I practically stomp the whole way there.

When I arrive, I walk through the door and two guys look at me, half amused and half horrified. And then I stop to think about what I probably look like. Jesus. I literally rolled off the couch after a sobfest and marched down here through the rain in sweats. I'm a soggy, sorry mess.

Then, right when I'm about to turn around and run the hell home, I see him.

And he sees me.

It feels like one of those moments where the music should sound behind me, lights brighten, and everyone in the background shimmers away.

He looks incredibly hot. His hair is pushed to the side, his jacket is off and his shirtsleeves are rolled up to his forearms, which I find sexy as hell. I watch as his eyes find mine, drinking me in as my heart pounds in my chest. My feet refuse to move.

And then he stands. He doesn't look at the blonde at his table, who is now turning around to see where he's going. He just walks. Right to me.

I want to scream, cry, throw something at him. Why has he turned me inside out like this? Why am I standing in a bar, dripping wet, like a crazy person? He's got me all mixed up and I don't know what to do.

I'm dying to kiss him. But that's what got us in this mess.

"What are you doing here?" he asks me quietly.

"I … panicking," I blurt.

"Why?"

"Because I'm scared!"

"Of what?"

"Of losing you, Reid." Tears fill my eyes and I swipe at them with the back of my hands. "This is exactly what I didn't want to happen."

"You haven't lost me, Wills."

"Then why have you been ignoring me for three days?"

He folds his arms over his chest. "I was just giving you some space to breathe."

A sob catches in my chest. "I can't breathe without you."

"And I can't be with you all the time and not want you." His voice is low and serious. "So we've got a problem."

Crying openly now, I bury my face in my hands and wish he'd put his arms around me. That's what a friend would do, right?

But instead of embracing me, he sort of rubs one arm like he's petting a cat. A sad, damp cat. "You should go home, Willow. People are staring. And I should get back to my table."

I lift my tear-streaked face. "Who is she?" I demand, trying to peek around him to see the woman he was with.

"Someone from work, not that it's any of your business."

The remark stings. "Is this your first date with her?"

"It's not a date. It's a work thing, and I have to get back to it."

"Leo said it was a date."

"Leo can be a fucking idiot sometimes." He pins me with his gorgeous blue eyes. "And so can you. I don't want anyone else, Willow. Why can't you get that through your head?"

With that, he turns around and leaves me alone in the middle of the bar, stranded in an emotional maelstrom. I'm happy he's not on a date, angry he just insulted me, turned on by his handsome face, torn by his words, and terrified I'll never feel his arms around me again.

I leave the building and walk home in the chilly drizzle, weeping softly the whole way. I miss him. I ache for him. I need him in my life.

By the time I reach our building, I know what I have to do. I have to risk it all.

CHAPTER THIRTEEN

Reid

I'M UNLOCKING MY APARTMENT DOOR, READY TO LET LOOSE on Leo for telling Willow I was on a date, when my phone buzzes in my pocket.

Willow: Hey. Are you home?

Me: Just getting in.

Willow: Do you have a minute?

Me: Sure.

Willow: I'll come out to the hall.

Frowning, I put my phone away. For a second, I think maybe she's come around, but not if she wants to talk in the hall. She probably just doesn't trust me in her apartment.

Her door opens, and she appears in a robe securely tied at the waist. Her hair is wet and combed, as if she's just showered, and her face is puffy but clean. She looks so pretty and sweet, I have to cross my arms over my chest to keep from embracing her.

"What's up?" I ask.

"I wanted to apologize about tonight. I was out of line to show up like that."

I shrug. "I'm used to it. At least you didn't hide behind a plant this time."

Her cheeks go a little pink, and she looks down, shuffling her bare feet. "I guess that was out of line too."

"Maybe just a little."

We laugh together, and it feels good. God, I've missed her.

"Did you have a nice evening?" she asks.

"It was okay."

She nods and tucks her hair behind her ears. "So, I've been thinking about it, and I understand why you've stayed away this week. Under the circumstances, a little space was probably the best idea."

No, it wasn't. But I don't want to argue with her.

"Anyway, I was wondering if you could do me a favor."

"What?"

"I know you said you had no interest in going on any more dates, but would you—"

"No." Turning around, I stick my key in the lock again. "Goodnight, Willow."

"Wait a minute, Reid." She takes me by the elbow and forces me to face her again. "I wouldn't ask you if it wasn't important. I know how you feel about being set up, and I respect that. But this would mean *everything* to me."

"Why?"

"Because if I don't at least appear to succeed with you, my mother is going to sell the business out from under me. I might not be the best matchmaker in the world, but I'm not ready to give up yet. I like my job. I need it. And besides." Her eyes light up, and she gives me a shy smile. "I have a feeling about this girl."

"A feeling?"

"Yes." She puts a hand over her heart. "You know me. I don't get feelings like that—the ones you can't explain that seem to come out of nowhere and stick in your gut."

"No, you don't." It's exactly how I feel about being with her, and more than anything, I wish she felt it for me.

"Well, I have one now. Please do this for me. Just meet her. If she's not your perfect match, I swear to you I will give up this fight, tell my mother I was wrong, and accept defeat." She clasps her hands beneath her chin and gives me an adorable, pleading look, her brown eyes wide and shining. "Please, Reid? Give me one last chance?"

I groan, knowing I can't resist her when she makes that face. I'm too crazy about her. "Fine. I'll give you an hour tomorrow night."

"Yay! Thank you!" She claps her hands and gives me a quick peck on the cheek. "I'll text you details tomorrow."

It makes me glad to be the one to put a smile on her face again, but I wish the circumstances were different. There is no woman alive that compares to her, as far as I'm concerned. "I want it on record that I said from the start this is hopeless."

She lifts her shoulders. "Maybe you're wrong."

"I'm never wrong." I unlock my door and push it open, needing to get away from her before I do something stupid like kiss her again. "Goodnight, Willow."

I enter my apartment and shut the door behind me without looking back. Leo is on the couch watching an old episode of Batman and Robin and eating a burrito.

I grab the remote and turn the TV off, and he looks up at me in surprise. "Hey! I'm watching that."

"Why did you tell Willow I was on a date?"

He takes another bite from his burrito, chews, and

swallows, like I've got all the time in the world. "Because she needed a push, but not from you."

"You upset her, you asshole."

He shrugs. "This is a very upsetting situation. But the two of you are being stubborn and ridiculous, so I figured I'd step in to help."

"Well, you didn't. You made her cry."

"Pretty sure *you* made her cry," Leo says with his mouth full. "That's the longest you two have gone without speaking in years. Did you talk to her?"

"Yeah, we talked." I run a hand over my hair. "And I agreed to go on another date with someone tomorrow night."

Leo swallows. "Why would you do that?"

"Because I can't say no to her. Because it made her happy. Because if I can't be with her, I don't really care what the hell I do with my nights."

"And *she's* picking the girl?"

"Yeah. She claims she found my perfect match."

"Dude." Leo shakes his head. "You guys are so fucking weird."

The following afternoon, I get a text from Willow with details about my date.

> Willow: Please be at Geja's at 7 PM tonight. Your perfect match will be waiting for you at the table. Reservation is under your name.
>
> Me: Fine.
>
> Willow: Thanks, Reid. I hope she's everything you're looking for.

She can't possibly be, because she's not you, I want to text back.

But I don't. It's becoming increasingly clear to me that I need to give up this fight and admit I might have been wrong about her feelings.

I fucking hate being wrong.

So I'm not in a great mood when I arrive at Geja's, a fondue restaurant in Lincoln Park I normally love. I'm kind of surprised Willow chose it for tonight, since it's a place I'd consider *ours*. We always come here on our birthdays, and stuff ourselves until we're positive we're going to burst.

Inside the dark, candlelit restaurant, I give the hostess my name. While she's checking for the table number, I glance around, and it occurs to me that not only do I have no idea what this girl looks like, I don't even know her name.

Goes to show how much I care about this date, I suppose.

But when the hostess smiles and asks me to follow her, I run a hand over my hair and make an effort not to look sad or angry. It's not this girl's fault things are such a mess with Willow.

The hostess leads me toward a wall of cozy, intimate booths lined with red curtains. "Here you are," she says, gesturing toward the last one.

The woman seated there turns to look at me, and my knees nearly buckle.

It's Willow.

"Hi," she says softly, with a smile that melts my heart like butter. Then she holds out her hand. "Reid Fortino, meet your perfect match."

I'm dumbfounded. For a full ten seconds, all I can do is stare at her. Finally, I take her hand in mine. "It's you."

"It's me."

Without letting go of her hand, I slide into the seat across from her. "I don't understand."

Her smile widens as she shrugs. "You were right. I do have feelings for you. I was just too scared to admit it." Then the grin turns mischievous. "But you were wrong too."

"I was?"

"Yes. You said your date tonight would be hopeless."

I laugh. "I did, didn't I? Well, fuck it. I was wrong."

"I love hearing you laugh. I missed it this week."

"I missed everything." I reach for her other hand and squeeze them both. "I'm so glad you're here."

"Me too." Her forehead creases. "But Reid, I'm still scared. I don't know where we go from here or what we're doing or how it will work."

"I don't either," I admit.

"I mean, we still have all the same issues. Those aren't just going to go away because the sex is good."

"The sex is better than good. The sex is fantastic. It will fix all our problems, wait and see."

She giggles. "I'm being serious. Tell me that no matter what, I'll never lose you."

"Come here." I tug on her hands, and she comes around to my side of the booth, where I pull her onto my lap. Wrapping my arms around her, I kiss her lips and rest my forehead against hers. "No matter what, you will never lose me."

"Promise?"

"Promise." I kiss her again and feel my dick coming to life beneath her perfect round ass. "But do we really have to stay for dinner? I haven't seen you naked in like five days, and I'm getting a little impatient."

"Yes, we really have to stay for dinner," she scolds. "I want a romance, Reid. Not just a fuck buddy. Can you give me that?"

"I don't know," I tell her honestly. "I've never been any good at it in the past, but for you, I'll try."

Her smile is worth everything. "That's all I ask."

CHAPTER FOURTEEN

Willow

H E SAID HE'LL TRY.

As I take my seat across from him again, my heart is racing in my chest and it's hard to breathe. I'm on a date—with Reid. I hoped he'd react this way. All day long I agonized over whether he'd show up or I'd be sitting here at the table alone. Now, I'm sort of dating my best friend.

Please God, don't let this be a mistake.

"So, our first date."

Reid grins. "Our first date."

The waitress comes over, smiles at him and then bites her lip. "What can I get you?"

This used to be amusing, the way women react to Reid—now, not so much. I clear my throat. "We'd like a bottle of Cabernet Sauvignon please," I say with a condescending tone.

He seems to understand what has me prickly and extends his hand across the table. I smile as I place mine in his. He doesn't even look at her.

"And you say you're not good at the romance stuff?" I tease as she walks away.

Reid grins. "I've watched enough of your crappy shows to know a few things."

"So, what I'm hearing is that they were not only emotionally riveting, they were educational."

"No."

"Well, look at us here. I'd disagree."

"You underestimate the power of me wanting to see you naked again."

"You know that just because we had sex once, doesn't mean we'll have sex tonight." Then I have to bite my tongue to keep myself from laughing at the pathetic look on his face.

"You're kidding, right?"

"Nope." I shrug and place my napkin on my lap. "I mean, this is our first date. What kind of message would I be sending if I gave it up so soon?"

"That you have pity on me and want to make me happy."

I tap my chin and look over to the left. "Pity sex, hmm. Doesn't sound too hot."

Reid chuckles once. "I wouldn't worry about that, sweetheart."

"Oh, now I'm sweetheart?"

"You can be anything you want."

A shiver of happy disbelief makes my spine tingle. "What I want is to enjoy tonight."

"Me too, Wills. I still can't really believe you're here."

"Who did you think was coming?"

Reid leans forward. "You know what, I didn't fucking care. I was praying for a no-show because I couldn't believe you were going to try to set me up after everything."

"Yeah. No matter what I tried to tell myself, I couldn't bring myself to do it. I may end up working for my sister, but I couldn't endure seeing you with someone else, let alone arranging it. And we both know I'm not too good at the whole matchmaking thing."

"I think you did just fine."

I laugh. "I ended up setting you up on a date, hiding in the ferns—with my sister as my accomplice—and then sleeping with you."

His eyes fill with warmth. "Again, fine by me."

"Seriously, the sex again?"

"Always."

Such a man. A sexy, smart, amazing man I can't get enough of. "You're incorrigible."

"No, I've just missed you."

"I missed you too. That was the hardest part. Knowing you were right there, across the hall, and yet you felt miles away. I had to fight the urge to knock on your door every night."

"I knew you'd come around."

I can't even argue with that. He probably did know. However, I wonder if he's not plagued by the same fears that I am.

Will we be okay if this all falls apart? Can we really endure taking this relationship further only to have it go up in flames?

"Hey." Reid squeezes my hand. "Stop that."

"Stop what?"

"That being in your head and making up worst case scenarios."

Jesus, this is going to be annoying. "*You* stop being in my head."

He shakes both hands gently. "Listen, if you doom this from the beginning, guess what's going to happen? We'll fail. Not because we're not good together, but because you already put that shit out into the universe."

Now I laugh. "You sound like Aspen with your universe talk."

"Well, even a broken clock is right twice a day. Maybe she's got a point, and that's why she and your mom get this whole matchmaking thing."

"And why I suck at it?"

"I didn't say that. And look—you did match me. We're sitting here, holding hands, on a date that neither of us planned to be on."

"Well, I kind of planned it."

He grins. "I've got plans too."

"Mind out of the gutter, Reid."

"Wills." He sighs. "This is the best first date I could ever hope for. First, we know that we like each other, we've been friends for a long ass time. I don't have to pretend I want to know all about your family, your cat, or whatever the hell crazy shit you'd say."

"I don't have a cat. I have plants."

"I'm saying that we get to skip all the things that men really hate. I already know that you're smart, funny, you can cook, and we don't have a thing to worry about in the bedroom. Do we have shit that we need to figure out? Yep. Am I worried about it? Nope. Just relax, please. Don't start going ten steps ahead of this. Let's take it day by day."

"Day by day." Just saying the words makes me itch. I don't know how to do that, but he's right. We already know each other's best and worst. There are zero issues with him making himself at home with me, and he gives multiples.

I just have to let go.

We're walking back to our apartments, his arm around my shoulder, my arm around his back, as though this was how it was always meant to be. We fit—perfectly. And our date is perfection.

After that initial talk about my fears, we settled down into just being Willow and Reid. He told me about the account that he got yesterday and I told him about Aspen's theories on stars and planets.

It was only a few days that we went without talking, but I felt like I missed so much. Of course, we also managed to gorge ourselves on fondue, so instead of taking a cab, we're trying to walk off some of the calories. Plus, it gives me a reason to touch him like this.

Which I like … a lot.

"Should we get ice cream?" he asks.

I nod, even though I'm stuffed. "You know I'll never say no to that."

"Oh, I know. Don't think I didn't realize last month when the half gallon I bought disappeared from my freezer."

"I don't even feel bad about that. You steal my food all the time. And in my defense, Leo gave it to me without a fight."

"He's dead to me."

I slap his chest. "You know, you should be nice to him. If it weren't for him telling me you were on a date, I would probably never have had the balls to accept what I was feeling for you."

Reid looks down at me with a grin. "And what are you feeling?"

"Well, I feel like this was a really good first date. And I never want it to end."

"That makes two of us."

"And do you think you'll be asking me on a second date?"

Reid presses his lips to my head. "I'll let you know."

I laugh once. "You're mean."

"You know who's mean, that one dude on This is Us! What the hell was he thinking by talking to that one chick?"

I gasp and stop walking, bringing him to a halt. "You watched it? On your own? Without me?"

His lips part and he rolls his eyes. "You left me off in the middle of a pivotal part. You weren't talking to me, so what choice did I have?"

"Oh, I can think of many, but watching the show you claim to hate isn't one."

"Whatever. You know, I actually enjoyed it without listening to your sniffling throughout. Although, Leo was fucking crying, and I would've much preferred comforting you to throwing the box of tissues at him."

I start to laugh and then shake my head. I am never going to let him live this down.

"Don't give me that look," he warns.

"What look?"

"The one you gave me just now that says"—his voice goes up a few octaves to mimic mine—"Reid, you're so sensitive, I knew you liked that show all along."

"Your words. Not mine. I was going to say that I'm going to plan a marathon for one of our next dates so we can catch up on the episodes we missed and analyze them in depth."

He moves closer and I have to lean my head back to look at him. "The only thing I want to analyze right now is your naked body."

I grin because I really want that too. But teasing him is so much fun. "Not until you admit the truth."

His head drops slowly and my heart begins to pound harder in anticipation. I have to hold out though. No matter how much I want to feel his lips on mine, I'm going to remain strong. His admission is my victory.

"What truth?"

"That you like the show …"

"I like you." He drops a little lower. "I like your lips. I like the way my name sounds on them. I like that right now, your eyes are telling me you really want to kiss me and that's the damn truth."

I like that truth, too, but it wasn't what I was looking for. "Close, but …"

His lips are a breath away now, my breathing is accelerated and I don't think I can hold out. I need to kiss him. "Are you going to deny me, Wills?"

I don't think I could deny him anything when he's like this. His cologne, his breath, his heat is all around me. Reid is the only thing that I can feel, see, smell, and hear. God, I could drown in this man and never come up for air.

"Are you going to admit it?" I ask as my last thread of self-restraint snaps.

I can feel his smile against my lips. "Kiss me, Willow and I'll tell you anything you want to hear."

What were we talking about again?

I don't even remember, and honestly, I don't give a shit. All I care about is him.

My hand reaches up around his neck, and I push up on my toes, bringing our lips together. Reid's arm tightens, and then I'm flush against his body.

He may have asked for me to kiss him, but he's in control of this. I let him lead, here on the busy street of Chicago, not caring who walks by or sees. His tongue slides against mine in the most delicious way. I moan, holding him tight, not wanting it to end.

Reid pulls back all too soon. My breath is coming in short puffs and I have a death grip on his arms.

"What was it you wanted me to say?" he asks, his voice deep and raw.

I try to get my brain to start functioning again and once I think I can form words, I smile seductively. "That you want to skip ice cream and come back to my place."

"Good because I have something else I'd like to lick."

CHAPTER FIFTEEN

Reid

I DON'T THINK THE WALK TO OUR APARTMENT BUILDING HAS ever felt so damn far. She wore the freaking boots with the high heels, which I love, but they're slowing us down. I'm half tempted to toss her over my shoulder.

Jesus Christ, has there ever been a more intense kiss between two people? No. I don't think there has.

Each second that passed between us only made the anticipation better. However, I don't know how the hell I'm going to control myself.

I want her more than anything. I've thought of this moment since I had a taste of her and now, I want to feast on her.

"If it wasn't so cold, I'd take these damn boots off and run," she says, trying to walk faster.

"Yeah? Why is that?"

She giggles softly. "Oh, I don't know, because I wish we were up in my apartment already."

Glad to know she feels the same. "What exactly do you wish we were doing, Wills?"

I'm only torturing myself right now, but I remember what it was like when she let herself go last time.

"You want to know?"

"I want to hear it because once we're inside that damn door, all bets are off. I'm going to strip you down and my mouth is going to be all over you. You won't even be able to think, let alone talk."

It's only fair she knows what's coming. Which will be her … many, many times tonight.

"Hmmmm," she says as I pull open the lobby door. "Let me think."

I follow her to the elevator and watch her hit the upward arrow. A moment later the doors open, and we get on with several other people.

Which is why it surprises me when she leans over to whisper in my ear. "First, I want to watch you get naked. I want to see how hard you are for me."

The answer is very hard.

Extremely hard.

Painfully hard.

And her words are making it worse. I have to adjust myself, which makes her laugh.

"Then I might like to get my hands on it," she continues softly. "You know. Play around a little." She puts a hand over my crotch and squeezes for a second. We're at the back of the elevator, so I don't think anyone noticed, but still.

A small sound emits from the back of my throat, and I turn it into a cough.

"Then I think I'd like to taste it." She gets even closer to my ear, so close I can feel her lips. "Lick it. Suck it."

The elevator doors open on our floor, and I bolt through

them like a rifle shot, dragging her behind me. "Yours or mine?"

She's laughing as she stumbles along in her heels. "Mine."

I stop in front of her door. "Open it. Right the fuck now."

She takes the key from her purse, and I grab it out of her hand, shoving it into the lock. I turn it, throw the door open, yank her through, and toss the key on the floor. "You were saying?"

Her smile says *come get me* as she backs into the living room. There's only one lamp on, so I can barely make out the fire in her eyes, but I know it's there. I'm walking straight toward her, my hands loosening the knot in my tie.

"Are you going to give me what I want?" she asks breathlessly, dropping onto the couch.

I want to rip that dress off her and ravage her in ten different ways, but there's something hot about letting her think she's the boss.

For a minute or two anyway.

I pull my tie off and throw it aside—not too far, since it could be useful later, especially if she really gives me trouble. Then I unbutton my shirt. Unbuckle my belt. Unzip my pants. I remove my clothing one article at a time, my eyes locked on hers. She watches my every move, her mouth falling open, her breath coming faster, her eyes going wide.

I leave my boxer briefs for last, and when I finally take them off, she stares at my massive erection and licks her lips.

"Does that answer your question about how hard I am for you?"

"Yes." She moves to the edge of the couch and runs her hands up the front of my thighs. Looks up at me. "And it's a very good answer."

"I'm a bit of an overachiever."

She smiles, her mouth tantalizingly close to my cock. "I can tell."

I'm about done with standing still, but then she wraps both hands around my shaft and rubs the crown over her gorgeous full lips. My legs nearly give out. "Fuck," I whisper, watching her tongue swirl across the tip.

My hands curl into fists as she licks me from bottom to top once, twice, three times, going slower with each stroke and moaning softly. I'm fighting the urge to put my fingers in her hair, hold her head steady, and fuck her mouth—I'm fighting it so hard, I clench my jaw painfully tight.

And then she takes me between her lips, sliding her hot little mouth down my hard length, and I groan in agony. The agony intensifies when she slips one hand between my legs and caresses me playfully. I stop battling the devil on my shoulder and fist one hand in the back of her hair as she moves her head up and down in a lazy, luxurious rhythm, a little deeper every time. When she finally takes me to the back of her throat, I can't even breathe. I don't know what the fuck she's even doing with her tongue, but it feels like the most magnificent moment of my life. My entire body is on fire, and I'm dangerously close to orgasm.

But I don't want her to stop. It's a side of Willow I've never seen—unabashed, smoking hot, totally confident. Yet she's vulnerable like this too. I'm standing over her with her head in my hands and my dick in her mouth. It gives me a sense of power, of being in command, and it shows how much she trusts me.

When I know I won't be able to hold back if she keeps going, I pull back. "You need to stop."

"Why?" she asks, panting a little. "Don't you like it?"

"I like it too much, and I don't want this to be over so soon."

"But we have all night." With a troublemaking gleam in her eye, she takes me back into her mouth again, and she doesn't stop until my legs go numb and my knees threaten to buckle and I'm cursing and growling and coming so hard in her mouth I don't know how she's not choking on it.

Finally, she collapses back onto the couch, breathing hard and wiping her lower lip with the back of one hand. Her expression is one of triumph. "Ha," she says. "I got what I wanted."

"You are a very bad girl, Willow Hayes. And I think you need to be punished." I lean over and reach for my tie.

She glances at it in my hands. "What are you going to do with that?"

"I'm going to tie you up."

She starts to giggle. Our eyes lock, and I can tell she thinks I'm joking. But then I get her by the wrist, and her laughter fades.

"Reid, you're not serious."

I smile villainously. "Try me."

Shrieking loudly, she jumps off the couch and slips past me, making me chase her around the apartment, which only adds to the game. I end up catching her in the kitchen, throwing her over my shoulder like a caveman, and carrying her into the bedroom. She squeals and pounds on my back the whole time. "Reid, stop!"

No fucking way.

I toss her on the bed, strip her naked, bind her wrists over her head, and tie them to her wrought iron headboard.

"What are you going to do to me?" she asks, and I can hear the slight tremor in her voice.

"Everything," I tell her. "I'm going to start with my hands, like you did. I'm going to touch you in all the right places until you're soaking wet."

"Oh, God," she whispers.

"And then I'm going to use my mouth, like you did. I'm going to torture you with my tongue and my fingers until you're desperate to come. I want to hear you beg for it."

She whimpers, a soft, breathy little sound that makes me smile in the dark.

"And then," I continue, whispering low in her ear, "after I make you come like that, you're going to beg for my cock inside you. And if you're a very good girl, and you say everything I want to hear, do all the things I want you to do, I'll give you what you want."

She arches and strains beneath me. "Reid, kiss me."

"I will, sweetheart. But first ... tell me what a bad girl you are." I am fucking loving this—it's going to take me a little while to recover anyway, so I might as well fill the time with something fun, right?

"I'm ... I'm a bad girl," she whispers.

"That's right." I press my lips to hers, stroking her tongue with mine. "A very bad girl."

The entire night is perfection.

Willow does everything I ask, and hearing those dirty words in her sweet little voice is unreal—it has me hard again in no time. But I do things exactly the way I planned, bringing her close to the edge with my fingers and taking her over with my mouth. She writhes and struggles against the tightly knotted tie, and her frustration at being unable to use her hands is hotter than fuck. It makes her use her body in ways I've never imagined—moving in ways that show me what she likes, how she wants it, when to go hard and when to ease up.

In the end, I free her wrists from the headboard so I can have the satisfaction of feeling her clutch and claw at me, pull me in deeper, fist her hands in my hair. I love that she wants me this way. I love the way her skin feels against mine. I love sliding into her tight, hot body and burying myself deep within her. It's like nothing I've ever experienced before, because it's Willow's skin, Willow's body, Willow's voice repeating my name until we're lost to it, exploding together in perfect harmony.

"I love you," someone says as we're catching our breath.

Holy shit. I think it was me.

There's a pause.

"What?" Willow whispers.

I say it again. "I love you." It's not like I haven't said the words to her before, but this feels different.

"I love you too." She says it kind of like we always say it, lightly. Affectionately.

"No. I mean I'm *in love with you*." I lift my chest off hers and look down at her face, wishing I could see her expression better in the dark.

"Reid ... are you serious?"

"Yes. I don't think I've ever said those words to anyone before, but I feel it—I'm madly in love with you."

And then, of course, she starts to cry.

"Um, that's not really the reaction I was hoping for," I tell her.

"I'm sorry," she says, sniffling, "but it's just really emotional for me to hear you say that."

"Because you finally made a perfect match?"

"No!" She slaps my chest. "Because I'm in love with you too, you jerk! I think I've always been in love with you. I just didn't know what to do about it."

"Same. I think I kept telling myself it was impossible, that you didn't want me that way, so it would never work."

"I did want you that way. This way." Her arms and legs tightened around me. "But I was scared."

"I know." I kiss her forehead. "Relationships are scary. But lucky for us, we know each other really well. There won't be too many surprises."

"Well, it kind of surprised me when you tied me up." She giggled. "Although, I have to admit I liked it. It made me think there are still things about you to learn."

"Good."

"So can I tie *you* up sometime? Give *you* a spanking?"

"Fuck no. I will do the tying up and spanking in this relationship."

She sighs dramatically. "Fine. I guess I'll just have to think up other ways to be naughty."

"That is a fucking deal."

God, I love my life.

CHAPTER SIXTEEN

Willow

I WAKE UP IN REID'S ARMS, THE WARMTH OF HIS BODY BEHIND me, the masculine scent of his cologne on my sheets. Smiling, I breathe it in without even opening my eyes.

For the first time in so long, I feel completely happy.

I took a risk, and it paid off. Do we have all the answers? Nope. But we'll find our way together. And I trust Reid to keep my heart safe.

He stirs behind me, and I feel a little tap-tap-tap on my ass. It makes me snicker, and even though I try to smother it, he hears.

"Are you laughing at my erection?" he asks, his voice gravelly.

"I would never," I say, putting a hand over my mouth.

"Good, because there is nothing funny about my dick. It is a very serious, very *large*, very important thing."

I burst out laughing. "Is that so?"

"Yes, that's so," he parrots, tickling my ribcage and making me shriek. "Do you want to *feel* how large and serious it is?"

I roll my eyes while shaking my head. "I think I got a good idea of that last night."

He beams. "You did, but maybe you forgot."

As much as I'd love to stay in bed and be reminded, I have to get up because today is my parents' anniversary party. "You can remind me tonight, affffter …"

"After?"

"After we go to my parents' party."

Reid groans, tossing his arm over his eyes. "That's today?"

"It is."

"Did you plan this?"

"Plan what?" I ask, completely confused.

"That you'd magically decide you love me and then remind me it was your parents' anniversary party?"

He's a special snowflake, that's for sure. "First of all, you agreed to go to this party months ago. Second, the only thing I planned was to find you someone to love—I had no idea it would be me."

Reid presses his lips against mine and then tosses me back against the pillows. My hands are in his hair, holding him to me. Kissing him like this is beyond words. It's fun and amazing and *weird*, because I never really thought it would happen, and yet … it's right.

We're right.

"Well, it is you." Reid hovers over me. "It's you, Wills."

"It's you too. Now," I tell him, pressing my hand against his chest and pushing up. "Let's get going."

"I would much rather get naked."

Same here, buddy. "Do you want to shower at your place and meet me?"

"No."

"Well, what's your plan?"

Reid gets to his feet and walks around the bed. Before I have a chance to ask him what the hell he's doing, he leans down and tosses me over his shoulder. I let out a squeak when his palm lands on my bare ass.

"Reid! Put me down!"

"Nope."

He marches into the bathroom, turns the water on, and deposits me on the edge of the sink. The granite is freezing, but when he kisses me, hard and deep, I no longer care. Our lips move together, each of us desperate for the other. He lifts me again, my legs wrap around his middle and he walks me into the shower, where his plan becomes very, very clear.

"Stop fidgeting," he tells me as we stand outside the door to my parents' lakefront home, where the party is being held.

"They'll know."

He takes my hand in his. "They probably already suspect you're not a virgin, Wills."

"But now they'll know for sure. They'll see it on my face or experience some sort of weird mind detection thing. You know my family is a bunch of wacko hippies who see through your soul. We can't go in there. Let's just head back."

Reid had to listen to me fret for half the ride. I wasn't nervous until we were about midway here and stuck in traffic. He started joking about how my mom was going to know we had sex since I can't stop smiling and he can't stop touching me.

Then ... I freaked.

My parents are cool, but I don't know how cool they'll

be about this. It's Reid. It's sex with Reid. Mom might be fine because she's all about love and intimacy, my dad … not so much. Not to mention, I'm still sort of reeling from the whole thing myself.

Reid and I are dating. We're the Ross and Rachel of our apartment and I'm sorting through a lot of feelings right now.

"We're not heading back," he says.

"I'm not going in there."

He lets out a groan. "We drove up here, it's your parents' anniversary, and you're being ridiculous." Reid rings the doorbell before I can stop him.

"I hate you."

"No, you don't."

I glare at him, pulling my hand away. "I could."

"Yeah, but you don't."

"I do."

He wraps his long fingers that do amazing things around mine and holds tight. *So much for not holding his hand.* His head leans down, eyes locked on mine. "I don't think you could hate me. I don't think either of us ever could hate the other. Now …" He smirks. "Relax so I can kiss you and remind you that you love me."

How can I relax when his lips are this close and I can almost taste him? I lean up, just a bit because now I want to kiss him. I want him to remind me because his reminders are the best. I no longer care that we're at my parents' house. I don't care about a damn thing but this man's mouth on mine, and then, right before we touch, the door opens.

Like a child caught with a hand in the cookie jar, I pull back.

My mother's eyes widen for a second seeing how close

our lips were, then looks down at our joined hands, and smiles. "Well, this isn't much of a surprise," Mom's voice is filled with an I-told-you-so tone. "But it did take you two long enough."

"Hi, Mrs. Hayes."

"Hello, Reid, my darling." She touches his cheek. "I'm glad to see you here."

"I ..." Reid pauses and then looks at me. "Wouldn't have missed it for the world."

Oh, please. We are not doing this game again. He plays my mother like a fiddle and she needs to know that all that charm is polished bullshit.

"He forgot, Mom. He forgot all about your big day. If it weren't for *me* reminding him, he wouldn't even have been here. He might've been holed up in his apartment, watching This is Us because he's a huge fan."

She snorts with a laugh. "I don't believe that for one second. Reid already sent us flowers."

"He what?"

"They arrived this morning. Thank you for the thoughtful gift, Reid."

When the hell did he send them flowers? He forgot until I reminded him. Then we went in the shower and I got ready ...

Oh, that bastard.

He's good.

I glare at him. "Well, it seems my boyfriend just thought of everything, didn't he?"

Wait, I said boyfriend. Holy shit. Reid is my boyfriend ... right? I mean, we're dating so that would be the appropriate term. We both already confessed we love each other, which would insinuate that we're exclusive and that this is really what we're doing.

I look up, my heart racing as I wait to see what he'll say or do, but he just smiles down at me. As though I'm some prize. Like the words that came from my mouth have given him some gift and I love it.

I love the look. I love everything that this is and the possibilities of what it could be. I love *him*.

"Yeah, he sort of did." Reid squeezes my fingers.

I didn't realize just how stupid I was about dating him until this moment. I was fighting against my feelings for him for what? To not have a chance to be happy? How did I not see just how his imperfections make him perfect for me?

Mom lets out a squeal. "And to think, you found a match for Reid and yourself all at the same time! Come inside, everyone will want to see you."

We enter the house, which is packed with their friends, and make the rounds. The entire time, Reid finds a way to touch me. It's sweet, and I secretly love every second of it. He's charming—as usual—and makes small talk with a few of my dad's business friends.

After an hour, Aspen finally shows up. She was giving homage to the mother earth or some shit.

I give up with her.

She gets smug the moment she sees us together. "Reid and Willow … who would've thunk it? It's not like there was any indication of it or anything."

I roll my eyes. "You don't have to gloat."

"Oh, but I do."

"I think we all knew this was inevitable after the attempt to be spies … really bad ones at that," Reid says with a chuckle and then wraps his arms around my middle from behind.

Aspen grins. "I'm such a good matchmaker."

"This wasn't your doing, Aspen," I tell her.

She shrugs. "I told you that the planets and universe were at work. There are some things that you can't fight no matter how hard you try. When things align, there's often an explosion."

Reid nuzzles his face into my neck, his voice is low so only I can hear. "I made you explode a few times."

Oh my God. "Behave."

"What?" Aspen asks.

"Nothing, just reminding Wills about the aligning of our planets and how there was a lot of big banging," he answers.

"Reid," I say between gritted teeth. Seriously, is he trying to make me turn red permanently?

"Oh, I'm sure there was," Aspen agrees. "You both have some major red aura going on around you. I'm surprised you haven't burned the house down with it or that it's not a little more orange since you worked it out. Maybe you guys just become this red when you're near each other. Did you satisfy her, Reid? If you didn't, it could explain why she's glowing now."

Someone kill me.

"What do you think, Wills?"

"I think I'd like for the floor to open up so I can fall into the abyss."

"It's a very serious thing," Aspen further explains. "If she doesn't find her release, the glow can become very troublesome."

"Stop talking, Aspen," I implore.

"We wouldn't want that, right?"

I swear, him taunting her is only going to make me hold out even longer. "You keep this up and you're going to be the one exploding when you sleep alone tonight."

Aspen shakes her head. "That wouldn't be fun. Release is a very important part of keeping the balance within yourself."

Someone in this trio is off balance.

"What are my girls talking about?" Daddy comes in and my cheeks are on fire. I pray he didn't hear any of that.

"Willow's sexual aura," my now dead-to-me sister answers.

Dad's jaw drops and he rubs his temples while Reid bursts out laughing. "Sometimes, I wonder why I even ask."

He walks away, muttering something about girls, and I slap Reid in the stomach and then my sister in the arm. "You know, he's a chemist, and he could kill you and make it look like an accident."

Aspen takes two steps back and then sinks to the floor with her legs crossed. "I need a moment."

"What is she doing?" he asks.

"She's resetting her gravitational something-or-other because it's off. She does this when she needs to have the Earth reconnect with her body."

Reid shakes his head. "And I thought Leo was a mess."

I nod. "He ain't got nothing on that one. Come on, it's going to be a while until she's found it. Let's go outside."

We head out to the patio, which overlooks Lake Michigan. So much of my childhood was spent here, and it always makes me happy to visit.

I rolled down the grassy hill, skinning my knee when I was six. I learned how to swim in this lake. The first boy I kissed was out on the dock three houses down.

"This is truly amazing," Reid says as he looks around. We eat cake and drink champagne, and eventually head back inside for a slideshow celebrating my parents' thirty-five years of marital bliss. When it's dark and the guests begin to leave, Reid and I grab a blanket and walk down to the beach. He sits in an Adirondack chair, pulling me onto his lap and wrapping the blanket around us.

"Is this weird for you?" I ask.

"What?"

"Us. Being a couple."

He looks out at the water and then back to me. "No, that's the weird thing. It's so easy and natural. As though we were meant to be like this. I almost think that when we weren't together ... that was the weird thing."

I know what he means. "You say stuff like that and I don't really know how to think."

"Why is that?"

"Because I don't want to fall to a place where I can never get back up again. I could lose myself in you, Reid. You're this ... this ... all-encompassing feeling. It's so much, so fast. Aren't you worried?"

His hand moves up and down my back. "I'm only worried that something is going to spook you."

"And I'm worried about the same."

"Then one of us has to promise to chase the other down."

I'm silent for a moment as I think about it. Being here where I have so many happy childhood memories, and celebrating my parents' marriage tonight, has me kind of sad that this might never be where Reid and I end up.

The ring, the wedding, the marriage, the family ... I still want it all, and he's afraid. I know the issues he has with his parents are tough, and he's against the whole institution of marriage. And right now I can say it's fine, I don't care, but what if he never changes his mind? What if I don't want to just be his eternal girlfriend?

Is all of that more important than being with him now?

I feel like I just got him. Do I need to worry about losing him already?

CHAPTER SEVENTEEN

Reid

"**S**TOP THAT," I TELL HER.

"Stop what?"

"Thinking."

Willow gives me a flat look.

"I'm serious. I can see those wheels turning in your head, and those wheels are not spinning in the right direction."

"I can't help it. Sometimes my wheels spin without my permission or my control. And I start thinking things that make me anxious."

"Don't" I wrap my arms around her and hold her tight, pressing my lips to her temple. "We're just getting started, Wills. Stay with me, right here in this moment, and let's just enjoy it for a while."

"But what if—"

"No buts. I refuse all buts." I squeeze her even harder. "Well, I should clarify that. I would be absolutely fine with your butt, and any time you'd like me to—"

"Oh my God. Enough. If you want me to enjoy this

moment, don't ruin it." She laughs a little. "You fiend."

"I can't help it," I tell her. "I'm pretty sure it's your fault."

"My fault! How do you figure that?"

"Well, you denied me for so long." I shift her around on my lap so that she straddles me, her knees on either side of my thighs. Immediately, I start to get hard. "I have all this pent-up desire for you. And I have to let it out, you know. Aspen said release is a very important part of keeping the balance within myself. You don't want me to be unbalanced, do you?"

"Now you're listening to Aspen? You've always said she was nuts."

"I changed my mind. When it comes to sex, I think she's right. In fact," I say, glancing around to make sure we're still alone on the beach, "what do you say to a little nookie by the lake?"

"No!" She looks horrified. "Reid, we're in public."

"No, we're not. I bet all the guests have left by now. And besides, it's October. It's too chilly on the beach for people your parents' age."

"Someone might see." She glances up toward the house.

"We have a blanket. No one will see." I adjust the blanket, which is big enough to form sort of a teepee from our necks down, holding it closed behind her. "Come on. Live a little."

She smiles, looking torn. "I want to, but ..."

"But what?" I ask, rocking my hips a little beneath her. She's wearing a dress, which would make this so easy.

"God, that feels good." She closes her eyes and moves over me, sliding her pussy along my erection.

"Doesn't it?" Keeping the blanket closed with one hand, I move the other down her back and over her ass, pulling her tighter against me. Our lips come together, and I tease her tongue with mine.

With a frustrated sound at the back of her throat, she puts her hands on my belt and unbuckles it. Ten seconds later, she's got my dick free and she's stroking it with her fist. "Can you be fast?" she whispers against my lips.

"Are you fucking kidding me?"

She moves her panties aside and gets up on her knees above me. Next thing I know, she's slowly lowering herself onto my cock until I'm completely buried inside her. "Oh God, that's deep," she whispers, her expression a mix of *fuck this hurts* and *give me more*.

As she begins to move up and down with small, rhythmic pulses, her eyes open and meet mine. Her breath is on my lips. Her body is tight and wet and warm, and I know I won't last long. Already I can feel my leg muscles becoming taut, heat unfurling at the base of my spine.

Her eyelids drift shut again, but I continue to watch her, amazed that this gorgeous, sexy, incredible woman is really mine.

"You're so fucking beautiful," I tell her as she picks up the pace. "You're gonna make me come so hard."

I'm already fighting it off, but I want her to come with me, so I do my best to think about other things until I can hear it in her soft moans and quick, panting breaths—she's close. Using my one free hand, I grab her ass and tilt my hips to give her the best angle I can, so the base of my cock rubs against her clit.

Thank fuck it seems to work, because I'm over the edge two seconds later, unable to hold back any longer, throbbing again and again inside her. She shouts my name once and drops her head to my shoulder, smothering her cries as her climax hits.

"Oh my God," she whispers right afterward. She picks up her head and looks around frantically. "Was I too loud? I was too loud."

"Relax. You were fine." I'm still experiencing little aftershocks and I hold her in place with one arm around her back, in case she was thinking of getting off me. "No one heard."

Once she's satisfied no one wandered down to the beach during our little interlude, she relaxes with a sigh. "That was really fun."

"Told you."

"I can't believe I had sex on the beach." She sounds proud of herself.

"See? We're good for each other. I'm going to help you loosen up, and you're going to—"

"I'm going to teach you how to cook."

"Um. What?"

"You heard me." She sits up and gives me her stern librarian look. "It's time for you to learn how to make dinner for yourself. And wouldn't you like to cook for me sometime?"

"Willow, there are *people* for that. Skilled people."

"Well, I want you to learn. What if I have a late night at work sometime? It would be really nice to come home and discover a hot meal waiting for me."

"Oh, I can give you a hot meal any night you want."

She rolls her eyes. "You're really not going to do this one thing for me?"

I sigh heavily. "Fine. I guess if you're offering to teach me, I should at least try. Will you wear a frilly apron and heels? And nothing else?"

One of her brows cocks up. "Don't push your luck."

"And where have you two been?" Aspen eyes us suspiciously as we walk into the family room. The guests have all left, and Willow's family is watching the slide show again.

"On the beach," Willow says. "We went for a walk."

"Is that what we're calling it now?" Aspen gives us a sly grin.

"Darlings, come sit." Mrs. Hays gestures to the open end of the large, L-shaped sectional. "Willow, you did such a nice job on this presentation. Thank you so much. I don't even know how you found some of these old photos!"

Willow smiles and sits down. "I have my ways."

I drop onto the couch next to her. "You haven't changed a bit, Mrs. Hayes," I tell her as a wedding photo comes on the screen. "You look exactly the same as you did the day you were married."

Willow's mom laughs and tosses her hair. "Thank you, you flatterer. Sometimes I can't believe it's really been thirty-five years."

"Just look at Dad's hairline if you need proof," quips Willow, prompting her father to throw a pillow at her. But he laughs along with everyone else, and it occurs to me how different my family is from the Hayeses. In fact, I can't think of one time when we all just sat in a room together and watched a movie, let alone a slideshow celebrating the love between our parents. If there were wedding photos, I never saw them.

I look over at Willow, who's smiling and laughing at photos of Mrs. Hayes when she was pregnant. "Look at that belly," she says. "Holy cow, you were huge."

"Well, you weighed nine pounds," Mrs. Hayes reminds her. "You took up a lot of space."

The smile stays on Willow's face as we watch the family grow from two to three, and finally four with the birth of Aspen. I see photos of Willow growing up that I've never seen before—adorable baby pics, gap-toothed elementary school portraits, awkward teenage photos, a family shot at her high school graduation. The final photo in the slideshow is a picture I actually took of the Hayes family at Willow's birthday dinner last spring.

Mrs. Hayes sighs. "What a beautiful journey it's been so far. I wish the same for both my girls."

"I wish to go to bed," says Willow's dad, rising from the couch. "I'm beat."

"Same," says Willow. "Mom, we thought we'd stay over rather than drive back. Is that okay with you?"

"Sure, honey." Her mom smiles at us. "Your room is all ready for you."

"Thanks."

"And don't worry about making noise tonight, your father sleeps like a rock."

"Mom!" Willow rolls her eyes. "Jeez. We're not going to make any noise tonight."

"They already made noise," says Aspen. "That's why they went for a walk." She makes little air quotes around the word *walk*, and Willow throws a couch cushion at her.

"Come on, Reid. Let's say goodnight before my family embarrasses me any further." She grabs my hand and pulls me from the room. "Goodnight, family."

"Goodnight, family," I say over my shoulder.

"Goodnight, dears!" calls Mrs. Hayes.

We head out to the car to grab our overnight bags and head straight upstairs to Willow's room. I've stayed at this house a bunch of times before, but never in the same bedroom with her.

She shuts the door behind us. "Sorry about that. My family can be kind of ridiculous."

"I think it's nice you guys are all so close."

"That's one way to put it." Smiling, she balances with one hand on the dresser as she slips off her heels. "I wouldn't trade my mom or sister for anything, but sometimes they drive me nuts. I don't know how my dad puts up with them."

"He loves them." I untuck my shirt and start to unbutton it. "It's obvious."

"Yeah." She pulls her dress over her head and opens the closet.

"I mean, thirty-five years." I shake my head. "That's amazing. I don't think my parents' marriage was even good for thirty-five days. They hate each other."

"Why are they still married?"

I shrug. "My dad always said it was cheaper to keep her."

She gives me a look over her shoulder as she hangs up her dress. "Come on. They had two kids. There must have been love there at some point."

"Well, there was sex at least twice." I sit down on the double bed and take off my shoes. "But that's all I know for sure. I've never even seen a wedding picture."

"Really?" Willow's eyes widen as she digs through her bag for her pajamas. "What do you think happened to them?"

"Who knows? My mother probably burned them, then stirred the ashes into her martini. God knows the woman doesn't have a sentimental bone in her body. And my dad's even worse." I stand up and finish getting undressed. "I bet there are no surviving pictures from when Leo and I were young."

She takes off her bra and slips on a big T-shirt. "Really? That's so sad."

"I remember lying in bed at night, listening to them scream at each other and wondering if they even loved us. The next morning, my mother would be too hung over to get out of bed, and I'd have to make lunches for Leo and me, make sure he had his homework in his backpack, make sure he got to the bus stop on time." The thought of it makes my stomach muscles clench. "It was fucked up."

She looks over at me, silent for a moment. "No wonder you've never really wanted kids. I guess I didn't realize just how unhappy your childhood was. I'm sorry, Reid."

"It's okay." Because I can't stand to see her looking sad, I go to her and wrap her up in my arms. "We made it through, and even though there are a lot of mornings with my brother where I feel like nothing has changed in twenty years, I'm not damaged."

"Okay," she says, pressing her cheek to my chest. I'm not sure if she believes me or not.

Actually, I'm not even sure I believe me.

We finish getting ready for bed and crawl beneath the covers together in the dark. Willow snuggles up to me and puts an arm over my stomach. "I can't stop thinking about what you said. About your parents."

I let my hands wander beneath her pajamas. "Want me to distract you?"

"Reid!" she whispers. "Stop that!"

"Why? Your mom said it was okay."

"My mom is not the boss of me."

"Actually, Wills ..."

"Oh, hush. You know what I meant." She tugs her shirt back into place. "She's not the boss of my sex life."

"Can I be the boss of your sex life?" I easily flip her onto her back, pinning her wrists to the mattress. "If the position is open, I would like to submit an application."

She sighs. "You're relentless."

"You adore me."

Her smile is slow and sweet. "I suppose I could consider your application, as long as it's very, very quiet."

"I can be as quiet as you can," I tell her, pressing my lips to hers as my cock grows harder between us.

She giggles and wraps her legs around me. "Then we're in big trouble."

CHAPTER EIGHTEEN

Willow

"HEY, YOU. WHY SO QUIET?" REID ASKS, glancing at me from the driver's seat. We're on the road back to Chicago from my parents' lake house.

"No reason," I tell him.

"Liar." He pokes me in the side.

"Maybe I'm tired. You kept me up half the night, remember?"

"Oh, yeah. That was fun being quiet."

"Um, we failed at quiet. Did you not see my mom and sister elbowing each other all through breakfast and my father doing his best not to look either of us in the eye?" I cringe at the memory. "Ugh. Brutal."

"He'll live. Now what's on your mind?"

"Nothing. Really." It's totally a lie, and I feel bad about it. I'm not in the habit of lying to Reid. But the truth—that I can't stop thinking about what he told me about his childhood—would probably upset him. I want to know more, but

I don't want to dredge up unhappy memories.

On the other hand, I don't seem to be able to let it go.

"Willow, I've known you for how long now?"

"Almost three years."

"And in those three years, how many times have you really been able to fool me?"

I shrug. "A lot."

"No." Reid lets out a laugh. "You only *think* you have, but you haven't. I see through all your crap. I consider it a gift from my father ... being able to read people."

I exhale, my shoulders slumping. "I just hate that you had the childhood you did."

He takes my hand in his. "I do too, but it is what it is."

Still, it doesn't mean that he deserved that kind of life. "I keep picturing you and Leo being small and dealing with your family fighting. It was just so different than the way I grew up."

He nods. "It wasn't fun, but Leo and I did fine. Well, I did, and I'm working on my brother. Now you know why I don't talk to my parents. They're a fucking mess."

Reid and I have always been open, but when it comes to discussing his family life, he sort of shuts down. Now I know why.

"Does Leo talk to them?"

He sighs with a groan mixed in. "Yeah, and that's part of the reason he's a goddamn mess. My mother is Leo's weak spot. She's selfish, conniving, and a raging alcoholic. Whenever she's on a bender or my father has said some horrible shit to her, she calls him."

"And he always answers?" I guess.

"Yep. Every single time. He's so damn desperate for my mother to love him, which I don't even think she's capable of doing. When it comes to my father, I think Leo's sort of over trying to change his mind. Dad told him he was a useless waste of space a few years back." Reid laughs once, but there's nothing funny about it. "We're both the children Vince Fortino wished he never had. If I'd taken the job at his company he was grooming me for, he'd probably tolerate me better, but fuck that. I swore I'd never work for him."

Reid's fingers turn white from gripping the wheel so tight. There's tension practically radiating from his body and now I regret telling the truth about my thoughts. My hand presses on his shoulder and then he starts to relax with my touch. "We don't have to talk about this."

His eyes meet mine. "No, you should know what kind of bastard I could become."

Now it's my turn to laugh. "You're not a bastard and you're not your father, Reid. I've known you for a long time and you would never treat people like that."

"Thanks." His smile is small and skeptical, and it makes my heart ache. I wonder if anyone has ever told him just how amazing he is. Does he know how smart, funny, sexy, and special he is? Did anyone love him for the man he is and could be? I don't think they did, and for that, I'm sad and angry. Reid deserved more than what they gave him. I plan to love him enough for all of us.

"I've worked really fucking hard to be nothing like him. But sometimes I worry it's inevitable."

"It's not. You'll never be like him." I rest my head on his shoulder, falling into a comfortable quiet as he drives back to Chicago.

I want to bottle this moment up and keep it close. There are so many words to describe what's in my heart, and they move so fast through my mind it's hard to keep up. I'm happy, loved, hopeful, and relieved, but also scared, worried, and curious on how we'll weather all the storms to come.

Mostly, though, I'm content.

"This weekend meant a lot to me," I say as we pull into the underground parking.

"You mean a lot to me."

Damn him for making me blush. "Well, that's a good thing because we both know how I feel about you."

He parks and grins. "Yeah, how's that?"

"Hmm, it's so strange, the first word I thought of was irritated."

Reid laughs. "So just like any other day."

"Pretty much."

"Good to know that things aren't going to change just because we're dating."

I shake my head. "Things most definitely are changing."

"Yeah, maybe you're right." He pops the trunk and grabs both our bags.

Sounds silly, but I love the little things like that. While it might not seem like much to anyone else, it's the world to me. It shows that he wants to take care of me in some way, and he's really always done it. He carries my bags, opens the door, and finds ways to touch me whether it's holding hands or resting his palm on the small of my back. I hope that never stops.

"I am," I tell him as we walk toward the elevators. "You're going to start cooking for me, that's a change. And we're sleeping together, which requires you and I to stay at each other's place a few times a week."

"Or every fucking night," he suggests, setting down my bag to hold the door open for me.

"We just started dating," I remind him. "No need to rush."

"I'm not rushing." He looks at me seriously. "I don't want to spend a night without you, Wills. Why would I?"

My heart thumps happily. "Don't you worry that we're going to want to kill each other?"

Reid lets out a huff that borders on a laugh. "Sweetheart, I've wanted to kill you daily, but I'm pretty sure you've felt the same thing with me."

"Wait! *You've* wanted to kill *me*?"

"Wills." His voice is soft. "It's only because I wanted you in other ways but lied to myself."

"Oh, well, that's a good answer."

He chuckles as his lips move toward mine. "I'd much rather do other things."

"Like?"

Reid's nose brushes against mine, his warmth cocoons me as his mouth is so close to mine. "Hmm ... there are so many options." He toys with me by not giving me what I want— him. "I could kiss you."

"You could."

"I could, but I could do other things too."

"I could tell you no."

Reid chuckles as if we both know that's ridiculous. "Do you want to tell me no?"

"Depends on what you're wanting to do."

I'm not going to let him think he calls all the shots. A woman has to keep her wits about her and all.

"I could tie you up again."

Warmth floods my core as I remember just how hot that night was. I've never considered myself very adventurous in the bedroom, but there was something about being with him

162

that made me open to it. I knew I could trust him. He would never hurt me, make me feel unworthy, or lie to me. For a control freak, it was sort of liberating to give him that power for just a bit.

"I might like that."

Reid's lips brush against mine. "I know I would like it."

"I bet you would. Kiss me," I tell him.

"Yes, ma'am."

His lips press against mine and I groan. How is it that we just had each other earlier this morning and I'm already desperate for him now? It's like this man is turning me into a sex fiend. His kisses give me air. His touch gives me life. His heart gives me hope. I want everything that he's willing to share because it's Reid.

All of him.

I want the good, the bad, and the ugly with him.

His hands fist in my hair, holding my lips to his as he kisses me deeper. I don't care that we're in the elevator and the doors could open at any minute. All that exists in this world is us.

Much too soon for my liking, we reach our floor and he pulls back. But as soon as we step into the hallway, he drops the bags and takes my face in his hands. His forehead rests on mine. "I don't know how I ever lived without you like this, Wills."

I touch my hand to his cheek. My heart is pounding in my chest because it's not what we didn't have before, but what losing this could do to me going forward. I hear my mother's advice to her clients in my head like a soundtrack, each piece of wisdom conflicting with the next.

Don't rush things, let them happen.

You can't love too hard, there's no such thing.

Stop trying to control the heart, it doesn't listen.

Fight for what you want because it won't be yours if you don't.

Don't fall in love with the potential.

Just because a person is right or perfect for you, you may not be the right one for them.

Speak the truth and it shall become real.

Our eyes are locked on each other and the last one of my mom's mantras gives me the strength to tell him what's in my heart. "I don't ever want to know what it's like to live without you like this again. I love you and I don't ever want to lose you."

Reid's fingers interlace with mine, bringing my hand down. "You won't. Somehow, I'll be a better man for you, Wills. Just give me time … and a lot of patience."

Patience, I can do. It's the time part that worries me.

CHAPTER NINETEEN

Willow

"WHAT ARE YOU DOING TONIGHT? WAIT, don't even answer that because I have a feeling I know exactly who and what you're doing," Aspen says as she flops into the chair in my office.

"Reid mentioned dinner, but I'm not sure."

"Is he going to cook for you again?"

I sigh heavily, recalling the accidentally blackened chicken and mushy, overcooked pasta he'd made the other night. "Let's hope not. I've changed my mind about him learning to cook."

"Was it that bad?"

"Worse," I confirm. "He was a terrible student and barely tried. I've decided I'll make the meals from now on, and he can take me out to dinner occasionally." I grab my phone and shoot him a quick text.

Me: Dinner still? Any ideas?
Reid: I'm in the mood for pizza.

Me: Sounds good. Where do you want to go?
Reid: Lou's or Pequod's ... you pick.

Like there's even a question of that. We both know who my favorite always has been and always will be.

Me: Is that even a choice?
Reid: I wanted to see if now that I've injected you with my essence you've come to the right side of the debate.

Oh my God. He's insane. But I still have to laugh.

Me: Your essence? Are you drunk?
Reid: What one of these words would you prefer? Junk, spirit of Reid, cream of king, juice of the ginormous rod, sperm of sex god, or maybe just my king's cum?
Me: I have no words for you. I'll meet you at Lou's where I'm sure you'll have come up with another hundred of these.
Reid: I'd aim higher, sweetheart. I'll see you around six.

I sit back, looking at the phone and grinning. He's such an idiot. A very lovable one that has turned my last two weeks upside down. Each time I think, okay, today he's going to piss me off or be bored of me, he's not. We click, just like we always have, but now we click in the bedroom too.

"We're going to get pizza at Lou Malnati's," I tell my sister. My stomach does somersaults thinking about spending the whole evening with him. We've both been so busy the last few weeks, we haven't had any real time together in days.

The last week has been especially, *insanely*, stressful. Reid is closing the deal on a new account at work and hasn't been leaving the office until about ten at night. Mom is working on a plan to assign the business over to my sister and me, and keeps us both here late.

While I would love to have full ownership, I have to admit that Aspen is a great addition. She's a lunatic, but has a knack for matchmaking that I can't deny.

"Can I come?" she asks.

"No, you can't come on my date," I huff.

"Why not? It's not like I'm going to lick him."

I'm not even sure what that freaking means. "That's reassuring, Aspen, but I haven't really seen Reid much and I'd like some time with him."

"I see, you have a hard time sharing your toys with others."

"No, I have a hard time not having you committed to the loony bin."

She shrugs and picks at the dead berries that she's sewn into her skirt. "Commitment isn't an issue for me."

"Just fashion then?"

Aspen sticks her tongue out at me. "Mock all you want, but my entire wardrobe cost what your blouse did."

That's not a bad thing. "If you're happy, sis, I'm happy."

"Good." She leans back in the chair. "Hey, did you ever call back that doctor?"

"Call what doctor back?"

"The one that called yesterday and was saying you had an appointment for tomorrow?"

I have no clue what she's talking about. Unlike my sister, I have everything documented and organized. My calendar gives all planning people an orgasm with how coordinated it is. Not wanting to stick my foot in my mouth, I open it up and look through. Nope, nothing for tomorrow other than I need to call and have my car serviced. Yes, I'm that thorough that I have a reminder to make an appointment.

"I seriously don't know what you mean."

"I wrote it down somewhere on your desk," she says as she gets up.

Aspen starts riffling through what was a very streamlined workstation, tossing papers around. I swear, I'm going to have hives if she keeps this up. "Are you trying to kill me?" I ask.

"Just close your eyes until I find it."

Knowing that she will just keep going, I do what she says.

"Aha!" she exclaims. "Found it!"

I groan, knowing that my desk is in total disarray. "Let me see."

Sure enough, when I open my eyes, my assumption is proven correct. Still, I grab the half sheet of a Post-It note with her scribble written: *fert clin conf call them 2 ch/can*

I frown at the message. "What on earth is this? It makes no sense."

"Yes, it does." She points at each hastily scrawled word. "Fertility clinic. Called to confirm. Call them if you need to change anything or cancel the appointment."

Fertility clinic! Immediately, I realize what happened—I deleted the appointment from my calendar, but I forgot to actually call the clinic and cancel it. My brain has been in new relationship mode for weeks. All I've thought about is hearts and unicorns and Reid's naked body in my bed.

"So what's the scoop? Are you going to the appointment?"

"I don't know." My heart is racing, and I feel backed into a corner.

I made this appointment months ago, before Reid and I were together. And I waited a long time to get in with this clinic because they're the best in Chicago. Should I cancel it? Or should I go?

Arguments on both sides start to battle it out in my brain.

I still want a baby. I've always wanted a baby and being with Reid hasn't changed that fact, has it?

But I know Reid doesn't want kids. He's made that clear and after learning about his family, I understand his position, but that doesn't really change mine.

A family is the one thing I've always wanted, in the depths of my soul. Being a mom, loving another, carrying a baby, and all that comes with that has been my dream. He wouldn't ask me to give up my dream, would he?

Maybe I should just go to the appointment, hear what they have to say, and decide later what to do. Going doesn't mean I have to do it, right?

But Reid will hate the idea. He's always hated it. And I can't keep this from him—I don't want us to have secrets. Should I try to talk to him first?

"What's going on with you?" Aspen asks, giving me the side eye. "Your aura is doing very strange things."

"I'm thinking."

"About nuclear disarmament?"

"About Reid."

She nods her head with a sad smile and then touches my shoulder. "You just went from a lovely shade of gold to very blue, my sweet sister. Don't worry so much, you'll find the right answers, you always do."

I wish I could be so optimistic. "I don't know, Aspen ..."

"Talk to me. Maybe I can help."

I look at my loopy sister and figure I might as well confide in her. Maybe the universe will communicate the right answers in her voice somehow. "You know how I've been thinking about having a baby on my own?"

"Yes."

"Well, now that I'm with Reid, I'm rethinking it."

"Because he doesn't want kids?"

I nod. "He's been nothing but honest about it."

"He also hasn't been in love like this before."

Maybe that's true, but I'm not naïve enough to believe that this profound love he's got with me is going to change anything this fast. It wouldn't be fair of me to think that either. "I don't think that he's suddenly going to want kids just because we're together."

"But he knows you want them, right?"

"Yes. He's been listening to me talk about it for months."

"So it should come as no surprise to him that you would still want to look into things."

"I guess not."

"You won't know unless you ask him."

I take a deep breath and blurt out what I fear. "What if his answer isn't the one I'm hoping for? What if my convictions about family are a deal breaker for him?"

Aspen looks sympathetic. "I don't know, Wills. All I know is that if you don't talk to him, then you're going to make up these theories in your mind, ones that are possibly, maybe even probably wrong, and then find yourself all screwed in the head over something you don't even know is true."

For once, my sister is actually making some valid points. "I'll talk to him."

"Good." She smiles and heads toward the door before stopping. "Oh! Also, when you want to talk about something important like changing his entire life views on marriage and babies, it helps if you're completely naked. Men are much less likely to object when there are boobs in their face."

And then she says something like that and I'm reminded that my sister is a nutjob.

"I'll take that under advisement."

She nods once. "Trust me on that one."

I lean back in my chair, thinking about what she said and praying that tonight, maybe I can approach it and he'll still be as supportive as he was before I fell in love with him.

If not, I might just try Aspen's approach.

CHAPTER TWENTY

Reid

"**A**RE YOU STAYING AT WILLOW'S AGAIN TONIGHT?" my brother asks.

"Are you staying here rent-free again tonight?"

"You can kick me out, but who would make sure the food gets eaten?"

I wonder most days if I'm not just enabling him, but then I remember that he's my brother and while my childhood sucked, his was worse.

"Yeah, eating the food is definitely an issue. It's a good thing I've got a mooch of a brother to take care of that for me.

Leo nods and then his arms go up. "Thank you for finally seeing it."

"Yeah, I see something all right. While you're eating left-over Chinese food, I'll be at dinner with my girlfriend and then eating her for dessert."

I leave that last one on because since Leo's girlfriend dumped him, he's been in one hell of a dry spell. He flips me off. "Asshole."

Damn straight I am. "You working tonight?"

His eyes shift around the room, not focusing on me. "No, I'm off. I'm … umm … I'm actually …"

This can't be good. The only time my brother stutters or has an issue forming sentences is when family is involved and whenever family is involved, I want to kill someone.

"What did Mom do this time?"

A sense of relief washes over him and he relaxes since he doesn't have to spell it out for me. "She's in rehab again."

"Oh, good, what do they say? Thirtieth time is the charm?"

"Reid."

As soon as he says my name like that, filled with disappointment and sympathy, my anger flares. Because he's not sympathetic to me—no, it's to her. It's to the mother that abandoned her kids to a revolving door of nannies and the monster that my father was. But Leo holds her as the victim and because I won't play their game anymore, I'm the bastard.

I've been killing myself to make sure my brother can find a way around the hell they've created, but one phone call and he's thrown right back in time. They're so selfish and unwilling to accept their issues. She's not in rehab because she wants to be better. She's in rehab so my father is forced to give her an ounce of attention. It's the same thing over and over.

Secrets and lies that keep manifesting in new forms, but always the same results. I'm done.

I've been done, but then Leo goes running back and it takes months for him to detach again. This is enough. "No, fuck that, Leo, you can't keep making excuses for her and thinking she's going to change. There is no change in that goddamn house. Mom will drink her feelings away while Dad fucks the secretary, maid, or whoever he can get his dick in."

"She's sick."

"No shit! They're all sick. They use each other and you in this game they play. You think Dad gives a fuck if she gets sober? No. Because then she might actually care about what he does at night when she's passed out drunk. If she cared about you at all, she'd let you go on with your life."

Leo gets to his feet and I wonder if he's going to deck me. "You know, Reid, you may have been stronger than me to walk away, but she's still our mother. She needs someone to fucking love her."

"And you and I didn't?"

"Yeah, we did and they failed us, but we're not kids anymore."

No, we're not, which means we don't have to take it, either. "You're right. I'm an adult, and I would much rather go across the hall to a woman who can show love and not require a damn thing from me other than loving her back."

"We don't all have a Willow."

I'm well aware of that, and I'm grateful every single day that I do. Still, I'm in kind of a shitty mood when I go knock on her door.

She opens it and smiles at me, easing some of the tension in my neck. "Hi, handsome."

"Hey."

She steps into the hallway, and I wrap my arms around her. Hold her close for a moment. Breathe in her perfume and try to let the scent and sight and feel of her make everything else go away.

"Tough day?" she asks, rubbing my back.

"The usual." Because I don't want to ruin our night with talk about my family shit, I release her and change the subject.

"You hungry?"

"Starving."

I take her hand as we start down the hall. "Me too. Let's go."

Lou's is busy, and we end up having to wait at the bar for a table. There's only one chair, so I give it to Willow and stand close beside her. She orders a glass of wine and I have a beer, and I love the way she sort of leans into me while we wait for our drinks.

"So tell me what's up with you," she says, looking up at me. "I sense a disturbance in the force."

I smile at the reference. "It's nothing much. I think I'm just tired."

"I *have* been keeping you up late. Sorry." Her grin says she's anything but.

I kiss the top of her head. "Don't apologize. Late nights with you are keeping me sane."

"Who's making you crazy?" She nods at the bartender, who's setting down our drinks.

I grab my beer and take a long pull, torn between wanting to unload on her on the off chance she'll have words to make me feel better and wanting to keep tonight sexy and fun.

In the end, sexy wins.

"Right now, you are." I lean down and whisper in her ear. "I can see down your blouse. Want to meet me in the bathroom for a quickie?"

She giggles. "At Lou's? I don't think so, babe. Let's save it for later."

"Damn. It was worth a try." I tip up my beer bottle again. "So tell me about your day. How are things going in the realm of happily ever after?"

"Good, I think." She tucks her hair behind her ears. "Aspen and I are learning a lot from Mom and, surprisingly enough, we make a pretty good team. She's better at the intuitive stuff and dealing with really emotional clients, and I'm good at the business tasks. I've also gotten more confident in suggesting matches, sort of letting my gut instincts guide me when choosing potential matches instead of being so dependent on what people say on their profiles."

"People probably lie a lot on those, huh?"

"They do!" She shakes her head before sipping her wine. "And I don't understand why—just say what you want. Tell the truth. It's not going to do anyone any good in the long run if you're not honest about who you are or what you're looking for."

I take another long drink.

"I mean, differences can always be worked out. But I think you have to know what your differences are up front. Then you can … you can talk about them if they become an issue. You know, if things go well." She lifts her wine glass to her lips again. "You wouldn't be … blindsided by something you never saw coming. You'd feel prepared to deal with it. Don't you think?"

"Sure," I answer, although I'm not entirely sure what she means.

"Excuse me, Reid? Party of two?" The hostess appears beside me holding two menus. "We have a table for you."

I leave some cash on the bar and follow the hostess and Willow to our table. As soon as we're seated, Willow starts talking again.

"For example," she goes on, not even glancing at the menu. "I knew from the very start that you didn't want kids. And you knew that I did. That I do."

"Uh huh." I look over the choices for toppings, although my stomach is bothering me a little bit. Maybe an appetizer would help. "You feel like some calamari?"

"Whatever you want. So I was thinking ... maybe we could talk about that."

I finish my beer. "About calamari?"

"No. About kids."

Setting my empty bottle on the table, I look up at her. Had I heard that right? "Kids?"

"Yes." She sits up a little taller. Fiddles with the edge of her menu.

"They're great. For other people. Or in small, small doses."

"But ... not for you? Like, ever?"

"Not for me. Like ever. Christ, I've got Leo living with me, probably for life. He's enough of a juvenile to deal with."

"Right." Her mouth turns down. It's obvious I've upset her, but it's not like my feelings on this subject could be a surprise.

"This is nothing new, Wills. Like you said—no blindsiding. I've never wanted kids and I've always made that clear."

"I know." She meets my eyes, her expression wistful. "I guess I was just hoping maybe you'd ... changed your mind."

A siren goes off in my head. "Are you pregnant?"

Her face blanches. "No! My God, no. It's not that."

"Good. I was about to have a stroke." In fact, the room is still spinning.

"It's just that I have that appointment at the fertility clinic tomorrow."

My jaw falls open. "What?"

"I have an appointment at the fertility clinic tomorrow. The one I told you about."

"I thought you canceled that."

"I was supposed to, but I sort of forgot." Beneath the table, she nudges my foot with hers and laughs nervously. "You've sort of hijacked my brain."

"So wait …" My head is foggy, and my throat feels dry. I reach for my beer, dismayed to find the bottle empty. "You kept the appointment?"

"Yes. But not on purpose," she says quickly. "I just forgot to cancel, and then yesterday I got a call confirming the appointment."

"So why didn't you cancel it then?"

"Well, I might have, but Aspen answered my phone and took a message—which she didn't even tell me about until this afternoon." She rolls her eyes. "Typical. Did I tell you what she was wearing today?"

I'm not in the mood to discuss Willow's sister right now. "So did you call back and cancel?"

"I couldn't. The office was closed by the time Aspen gave me the message. And besides," she says, taking a deep breath, "I waited a long time to get that appointment. I was thinking I'd keep it."

"Keep it?" Hot, pulsing fury surges through my veins. "You can't be fucking serious, Willow. You're not putting some guy's junk in you. I won't let you do it."

"Reid, keep your voice down." Willow looks around the restaurant in alarm. "People can hear you."

"I don't give a good goddamn who hears me. You are not going through with that ridiculous plan to have some asshole stranger's kid!" I know I'm embarrassing both of us, but I can't help it. What the fuck is wrong with everyone around me today? Am I the only sane person on the planet?

"Shhhh," she admonishes, her cheeks turning scarlet. "Can we please talk about this quietly? Calmly?"

"I don't know, Willow. I'm not sure I can remain calm when you're talking about having some other guy put his—"

"Will you please stop saying it like that?" Her tone gets a little sharper.

"How else am I supposed to describe it?"

"Why are you getting so mad about this?"

I stare at her in disbelief. "My girlfriend wants to let some other dick knock her up, and you wonder why I'm mad?"

"You said you would support my decision no matter what," she says, her eyes filling with tears.

"Well, that was before."

"Before what?"

"Before you were mine!" I hate how it sounds—possessive and jealous—but I can't fucking help it. "And if you want to stay that way, you're not going to that appointment."

Willow's lips press into a thin line, and she stands up. "You're being a total asshole," she says quietly, a tear dripping down her cheek. "I'm going home. If and when you decide you can talk to me like a grownup, you know where to find me."

I watch her walk away from the table, and it's as if every bone in my body wants to jump up and follow her, but every muscle keeps me pinned to my chair. This is the reason having a girlfriend doesn't work—they expect you to turn into somebody else. Willow has known all along how I feel about that fucking insemination shit. It was bad enough before we got together, but I can't believe she thought I'd be okay with it now.

The server comes by and asks if I'd like a drink, and I almost tell him no—but then I think, fuck it. I want another beer, and I can have one. Just because Willow took her toys and went home doesn't mean I don't deserve a drink at the end of what is turning out to be a really fucking shitty day.

"Thanks, but I think I'll go back to the bar," I tell him. "You can have this table for someone else. My date left."

"Sorry, man." The server gives me a sympathetic look.

"Don't be. I'm better off alone."

Angrily, I stride over to the bar, wedge my way in, and order a whiskey, neat. But I only get about two thirds of the way through it when I look over and see none other than my fucking father sitting there, with a woman who is not my mother.

Wouldn't luck have it that I'm forced to see him tonight?

He stands, making his way over to me. "Reid."

"Asshole."

Dear old Dad rolls his eyes like I'm a stubborn child, and maybe I'm behaving like one, but I can't think about that. It just makes me feel shittier about myself.

"Sorry to see your date storm off," he says, in a tone that lets me know he's more amused than sorry.

"I'm sure you are. I see you're on a date, though. Good for you. Glad to see some things never change."

Dad looks over at his table, where the brunette he's with is checking her lips in a compact mirror. "That's Veronica. She's my new secretary. I thought it would be a good thing to have dinner first."

First. He means before they go over his personal preferences for sex. "And after? What's for dessert?"

"Don't be an infant."

"Don't be a cheater."

My father laughs once. "I knew coming over here to talk to you was a mistake. You haven't changed. You're still a child, and I don't have the patience for it."

Well, color me disappointed. Like I give a shit. "How's Mom? Does Veronica like her? Or is Veronica the reason for her latest attempt at rehab?"

My dad throws a fifty-dollar bill on the bar. "This is for my son. He's had enough."

You know what? He's right. I have had enough. I've had enough of this conversation, of my asshole father, of feeling like a disappointment to everyone—including myself. And I have somewhere I'd much rather be.

I think of Willow's face when she left. The hurt expression. Guilt rips through my gut for the way I treated her.

Fuck, I'm an asshole. I shouldn't have talked to her that way. I shouldn't have embarrassed her like that. I shouldn't have acted like a goddamn caveman who thinks he owns his woman.

But dammit—all I wanted for tonight was to have a good time.

Then you should have told her that.

I look at my father, the man who has fucked my life up beyond compare, and shake my head. Then I toss the remainder of my drink back and slam the empty glass on the bar. "It's been great seeing you, Pop. Thanks for the drink. Now stay the fuck out of my life."

He grabs my arm, stopping me as I try to walk away. "You think you're nothing like me, don't you? You think it's going to be different with that girl? The one who walked out of here? It won't. Women are all the same, Reid. They want something, and they'll do whatever they can to get it. Then you're stuck trying to be someone you're not for the rest of your life. Someone you have no desire to be. Face it—like it or not, you're a Fortino man."

His hand drops, and I don't give him another glance. I walk away, desperate to be with the only person in the world who has *never* made me feel like a Fortino.

I'll do everything I can to forget I even saw my father's face.

CHAPTER TWENTY-ONE

Willow

I'M STILL SOBBING INTO A COUCH CUSHION WHEN I HEAR the knock on my door.

"Go away!" I yell.

"Willow, come on," shouts Reid. "Let me in."

"No!"

"Please?"

I sit up and sniff, wiping my eyes with the back of one hand. "Why should I?"

"I want to apologize."

Rising to my feet, I walk over to the door. But I don't open it yet. "For what, exactly?"

Silence.

I look through the peephole at him. He's fidgeting. "If you don't even know what you came to apologize for, why should I let you in?"

"I'm sorry I was a jerk at the restaurant. I'm sorry I yelled." He puts one hand on the door. "Please talk to me, Wills. I need you."

That tugs at me a little, and reluctantly I open the door. "Fine. Come in."

He looks relieved. "Thank you."

I step aside and fold my arms over my chest, because if he hugs me, I'm afraid I'll be too easy on him.

He goes over to the couch and drops onto it, rubbing his palms on his knees. Then he looks back at me. "Come sit?"

I hesitate for a moment, but then walk over to him. He grabs my wrist and tugs me onto his lap, then locks me into his arms so tightly I can't get up. After struggling unsuccessfully, I give up and sigh. "Fine. I'll sit here."

He rests his forehead on my temple. "Sorry I was a dick. I had a shitty day."

"I could tell. But you wouldn't talk about it."

"Because I didn't want to ruin our night."

"Um …"

"Yeah, I know. I ruined it anyway."

"Was it work stuff?"

"No. It's family. My mom's in rehab again."

My heart melts. "I'm sorry. But isn't rehab a good thing?"

"Maybe it was the first dozen times. Or even the first two dozen."

"You don't think she's serious about it?"

"She's never serious about anything except getting back at my dad. But she manipulates my brother so easily into taking her side."

"You prefer your dad's side?"

"I prefer my own side—which is the side Leo should be on, since I was the one who had to step in and raise him when my parents were too fucked up to do it."

I put my arms around his neck and settle a little more

comfortably on his lap. "I'm so sorry, Reid. Want to talk more about it?"

He frowns. "No. I want to be with you and forget anyone else even exists."

"We can do that."

"Are you still mad?" He kisses my chin, my jaw, my throat.

"I'm getting over it." I smile when his scruff tickles my neck.

"Good," he says, shifting me to the side and tipping me onto my back.

I want to talk more about what it was like for him growing up, but he's lifting up my skirt.

I want to talk more about his feelings regarding his mom's return to rehab, but his head is between my thighs.

I want to ask him again how he feels about my keeping the appointment at the fertility clinic tomorrow, but his naked body is moving over mine and he's pushing inside me again and again and all I can do is pull him closer and whisper his name and hope that being with me is the salve his soul needed tonight.

We go from the couch to my bedroom, and no more words are spoken.

When the sun comes up the following morning, I lie close to him and wish more than anything it could be like this for the rest of our lives. Going to bed together, waking up together, coming home to each other. Does he want that too? What does he see for our future? And what the hell am I going to do about that appointment? I don't have the heart to wake him up and ask him about it, but I don't want him to be upset if I go without telling him.

I'm completely torn.

I get out of the bed, and he doesn't stir. I need coffee and a plan—that's the only thing I can do right now. Once I get to the kitchen, I pour myself a cup, and sit at the table. There is nothing wrong with going for the appointment, is there? I'm not asking Reid to give anything up by me doing what I want in life.

There are things that happen in this universe for a reason, and that appointment not being canceled is a sign.

I drain my cup and hop in the shower. Once I'm dressed and ready, I check on Reid, who is still passed out. Waking him and talking about this entire situation would be the right thing, but I don't want another fight right now.

So I don't do it.

On a piece of notepaper, I leave a note: Went to my appointment, call you when I'm done. I love you.

I kiss it and pray he'll understand because losing him is my biggest nightmare, but having a family is my best dream.

»—♡—→

Once I'm at the appointment, my nerves settle down. I get checked in, pee in a cup, and have a full exam. Now I'm in the office with the doctor, going over everything and waiting to see the results.

My phone has rung four times, but I'm still not looking at it, because I know who it is and I'm a chicken shit.

The doctor seems optimistic, which is a good thing. "The process is simple, and it's definitely the more affordable option, compared to IVF," she explains.

"Okay. And how does it ... you know ... work? With picking a guy."

She smiles and pulls out a book. "We have a very good selection of quality candidates that have been screened. We take this very seriously, and always do our best to get a variety so that you have options. It's all in this book. Once you decide, we contact your choice, and then we do the procedure."

It sounds so simple.

"Then hopefully we get a baby, right?"

"Yes, that would be the goal, but you should know that it's not always successful one hundred percent of the time. There are a variety of reasons for failure, but I always like to be as upfront as possible. It may be a few times that we have to do this."

Oh, God. I don't know that I can endure it more than once. Not to mention that if I can get Reid to even understand it the first time, there's no way in hell he'll keep his shit together for a second. I feel dizzy and thirsty.

"Ms. Hayes? Are you alright?"

"I'm just a little overwhelmed."

The doctor nods. "I understand. Do your family and friends know about your plans? Do you have support?"

"Yes, my sister knows and my ... my boyfriend."

"Oh, you're dating someone?"

"I am."

I can see the confusion in her eyes. If I have someone, why would I want to have a baby with someone else?

"Is he infertile?"

I shake my head. "No, he's just opposed to having kids."

Her eyes turn soft and she clasps her hands in front of her. "Ms. Hayes, I want to be honest, this can be a very difficult route to have a child. People can fail to get pregnant or suffer losses. Even with success stories, it's the people around them that get my patients through it. I want you to be sure this is what you want, and also that the people around you will be there."

Will Reid be there? Will there even be an us anymore? After the way he acted last night, I don't really know. He was so angry that I would even think about this, but his position hasn't changed. Not once did he say he wanted kids.

I don't know what to do.

My phone vibrates and my stomach drops. It's as if he's been summoned by thought. I can almost feel the anger of the person calling.

"Thank you, Doctor. I really appreciate it. I have a lot to think about, but I know I want a child. That is the one thing I'm sure of."

"That's the one thing I can help you with. Here's the book. Go home, look at it, think it over, and then let's see you back here in a week. By then, I'm hoping you'll have a decision and maybe a selection for your donor."

My hands are shaking as I reach out and take it from her. "Thank you."

"I'll see you next week."

I nod. Yeah, I'll either be nursing a broken heart or Reid will have suddenly found a way to accept this.

I leave the office with my head spinning as I try to get a grip on everything. I have to talk to Reid, that's first and foremost. I love him. That much is true, but I don't think I can give up my dreams of being a mother—not even for him.

If it was Reid who wanted a kid, would I be mad if he did whatever it took to achieve that?

No. Other than him sleeping with another woman, nothing would be a dealbreaker. And I'm not betraying him with anyone. I'm just finding a way to have him *and* the child I want, if that's even possible. I'm not asking for anything from him, other than to love me enough to understand this.

As I walk, I grab my phone and sure enough, the four missed calls and two voicemails are him.

I play the first voicemail.

"Willow." Deep sigh. "I'm so mad right now. I'm so fucking mad that you went and you left me a damn note … and just … just call me back."

Second message.

"Wills, please don't do this. I'm not ready to … I can't lose you … just call me."

It's the tone of his voice in the second one that breaks me. He sounds desperate, sad, and disappointed.

I steel myself and hit his number. After two rings it goes to voicemail. Weird. Why would he want me to call him and then not answer?

He shoots me a text immediately.

Reid: Can't talk, in the middle of something at work.
Me: Okay. Can you come to my apartment after work so we can talk?
Reid: Yes. I'll see you about six.

That gives me the rest of the day to come up with some brilliant idea to keep him when I tell him I'm going through with the insemination. God, I hope I come up with something.

I have to.

189

I go into the office for the afternoon, but I find it tough to concentrate on other people's love lives. I keep hoping lightning will strike and I'll think of a way to have both Reid *and* a baby, some perfect combination of words to help him understand that being a mother doesn't mean I can't still be his. I can love him and love a child too, can't I?

Eventually Aspen wanders over. "I can't take it anymore," she tells me. "Your aura is a hot mess."

I roll my eyes. "Blue again?"

"Yes, but it's so muddy it's nearly gray." She perches on the edge of my desk and waves her hands around my face in some kind of woo-woo motion. "I sense fear. Indecision. Suppressed communication."

Giving up on work, I close my laptop and sigh. "That actually makes sense, believe it or not. I'm trying to think of a way to convince Reid not to bolt when I tell him I'm going through with the artificial insemination."

My sister nods thoughtfully. "The boobs didn't work?"

"Uh, they were a little too distracting. We didn't exactly have a conversation once boobs were involved."

"That can happen."

"But before that, we had a terrible fight. I told him I still wanted to go through with the appointment, and he let me know in no uncertain terms that he's totally against it."

"Did he give you a reason?"

"Honestly, I think it comes down to jealousy. He thinks by using a sperm donor I'll be having a baby with another man."

"Well, technically you are."

"But it's not like that at all!" I jump up and start to pace behind my desk. "That's just biology. It's not love."

"So why not ask Reid to be the donor?"

190

I stop in my tracks. "Reid?"

She shrugs. "Sure, why not? He's a little bougie for my taste, but his genes are probably solid."

"I know, but ..." I chew on my thumbnail a moment. "I don't think I can ask him. It will put him in a really weird position."

"What? Sharing a lifelong bond with you? Shouldn't he want that anyway if you're in love?"

"Yes, but ... I don't want to push. I feel like we just got to this really amazing place, and if I ask that of him, he could freak out and run the other direction. The whole reason I didn't ask him in the first place is because I didn't want to ruin our friendship. I was scared he'd feel pressured to say yes, and then it would be all awkward between us."

"But you're more than friends now, Willow. Things are different."

My stomach knots up. "I don't want things to be different. I thought I did, but now I'm scared."

"You need to let go of that fear, sister. It's holding you back." Aspen stands up and glides over to me, taking me by the shoulders. For once, she doesn't do anything strange—she just looks me in the eye. "Do you want Reid to be the father of your child?"

The thought of it makes my heart want to burst. "Yes."

"Then you need to ask him. Maybe that's what he's waiting for, Willow. A sign from you that he's the one."

For once, my sister might actually be right.

"Okay," I say, taking a shaky breath. "I'll ask him tonight."

CHAPTER TWENTY-TWO

Reid

THE AMOUNT OF EMOTIONS I'M BATTLING IS exhausting. I woke up after we spent the night trying to fix what I broke only to find that fucking note. Then, when I grab my phone to call Willow, I have two missed calls and a voicemail from my assistant that I need to come into the office and put out a fire.

Once I get there, the entire fucking world is falling apart because my client is an idiot and wants to change the entire plan we had laid out. Instead of having a big portion of the marketing budget go to social media, like I advised, he now wants print ads.

Then, I couldn't get a hold of Willow, but in a way I'm glad, because I was in no state to talk to her. Still, I spent most of the time looking at my damn phone, waiting for her to call. I willed it to ring, and then when it actually did, I sent her to voicemail because I didn't want to hear what happened at her appointment. Hell, I still don't.

When she says that she's going to go through with having

a baby, it'll be the end of what we have. We won't be able to find common ground. It doesn't matter how much I love her. I won't be enough. I promised her when we started this that she would never lose me, and I realize now what a fucking asshole I was to say it, because that's exactly what will happen.

She's going to go on with her life, raise her baby, and I'm going to be over at my place raising Leo. I'll have to move because I can't even stomach the idea of her pregnant by some dickhead. The thought alone makes me sick.

I get through the doors of our apartment building and head to Willow's. There is a note on the door, telling me to come in.

I open the door. "Wills?"

"In here," she calls from the kitchen.

The smells assault me—chicken, spices, tomatoes, and cheese. My stomach growls.

When I get in the kitchen, I can't even believe my eyes. The countertops and tables are filled with rolls, pastries, lasagna, stuffed artichokes, a salad, and she's frying what smells like chicken. "What's all this? Are you expecting people?"

"No. Just you."

Okay, I know I eat a lot but this is insane. "Right, well, you know that I can't possibly eat all this, right?"

"I know. I stress cooked."

"Apparently you're really stressed. I would much prefer another way to work it out, but I guess we all have our things."

She tries to smile, but then her lip quivers. "Are you not hungry?"

Like that's ever been in question. "I can always eat, Wills."

"Good, and then … after, we can …"

I finish her sentence. "We can talk about today."

I take a good look at her seeing how much stress is in her eyes. She's trying to fight it, but I know her too well. Then, after another heartbeat, a tear falls. Before I can take a step, she rushes towards me, wrapping her arms around my neck, and I hold her tight. The sound of Willow crying is like a knife to my soul. Knowing that I'm the one causing her tears makes it even worse.

"Don't cry. I can't handle it when you cry."

"I know. It's just that I'm scared."

"Of what?"

She cries harder. "I know how you feel and I'm trying to understand better because ..." She pulls back and I rub my thumb against her cheeks, wiping the tears that have fallen.

"Because?"

"Because I want us. I want it all, Reid. I want you and I want us and I want for it to be *us*."

I feel like she's talking in circles. "You want for what to be us?"

Willow takes a step back, she releases a deep sigh and then her eyes fill with resolution. "I've been in here for hours, cooking and flipping through this book of guys trying to find a father for this baby I'm going to have, and you know what I realized?"

I want to fucking throw something through the wall when I imagine her looking for a man who is able to give her what she wants because I won't.

"Don't say it," I command. "I don't want to know about some asshole donor who doesn't deserve to know you, let alone get you pregnant."

But Willow doesn't obey commands. "That's just it. I re-alized I don't want some donor's baby. I want yours. I want *you,* and I want a baby that has *your* blue eyes. I want to look at his or her little face and see resemblances to *your* nose, your mouth, your dark hair."

I shake my head because this is absolutely not going to fucking happen. "Stop, Wills."

"I want to hold a child that is equally you and me. I want to have this life with you because I'm so deeply in love with you."

Jesus Christ. She can't be serious. She only wants this because she doesn't know what the hell lives inside of me. The man I'm destined to be. Why would she allow that around her child?

"Willow, this can't even be an option. I can't possibly have a kid with you. I won't do that. I will never be a father."

"Why? Why won't you do this with me? I love you and you love me, Reid. It doesn't make sense to me."

Of course it doesn't. She grew up in the perfect home. She had two amazing parents who loved her and Aspen. They gave them things, not just material things, but love and support. In my home, we were only given what would further my parents' twisted game of manipulation. I saw how two people who loved each other became the worst versions of themselves and destroyed two kids in the process.

"If you grew up in my house, you'd understand. I won't be the father of your kid. I won't be the father of anyone's kid. I told you this. I told you how I felt about marriage and having a family."

She bites her bottom lip and fights back the welling moisture in her eyes. "I think I knew that would be the answer, but God, I hoped ..."

"Hoped what?"

"That this wouldn't be how it ends. I wished it so hard because I'm not ready to lose you."

I start to pace, pushing my hand through my hair. "Lose me? Why does this have to be the end? Jesus, Willow. You can wait. You can put this off, right? There's no need to do this right away."

She shakes her head with her lips parted. "Wait for what, Reid? You're not willing to even think about it. It's just no. So what am I waiting for?"

"Time! Just time together."

"I don't want to wait. I thought that maybe you'd see that this is the way we can stay together. Otherwise I have to give up the one thing I really want. I would have to find some way to accept that all I'll ever be is this."

"What the fuck does that mean?"

"It means, I'll be good enough, but never enough. I'll always be fighting this distorted version of you, the one who thinks he's just like his father. Which I would do, I would fight every day for the rest of my life if I thought I could make you see how wrong you are. You won't let me, though."

"Because you only know the man I allow you to see. If I married you, Wills, I would ruin you. I would become him, because that's who I am underneath what I let show."

Willow is so damn sure of me that she refuses to break or bend. "That's where you're so wrong. All I want is you. All of you. I want the good, the bad, the ugly and the wonderful parts. I want to wear a white dress and walk to you. I want to have a part of us growing inside me. I want to show you how you are nothing like your father. You are kind, compassionate, and you have the greatest capacity for love."

My heart breaks. Everything inside of me is tight because

I see the resolution in her eyes. She wants this. No matter what I say or do, there is nothing that will change. Willow wants her family and that includes a child. And now she thinks it should be me who fathers it. But I can't give her the one thing she wants, no matter how much I wish it.

Fuck.

"You want to believe that, but I could never love a child, Willow, because I was never loved as one. I don't even know what that looks like."

She wipes the tear. "I would show you."

I laugh once. "And I would show you a monster. I won't do it. I won't have a kid. I won't marry you. I told you all of this and you didn't believe me."

"Then that's that? There's nothing that will ever change your mind?"

"No." I can only control this.

"I always knew I wouldn't get to keep you," she says as she clutches her stomach. "I just didn't realize how much it would hurt when our time came."

She's being irrational. I have to find a way to get through to her, because this doesn't have to be the end. We can still be together now—she just has to delay her baby plan.

"Why does this have to end? Why can't we work it out? When the hell are you having this kid?" I know I'm going in circles now, but the finality of this is eating me alive. I'm desperate for some kind of option that buys us more time together.

"I can go next month to get started."

"Next month!" I shout. "No! You can't do this, Willow. You can't go next fucking month. Just give me six months. A year. Then … then, I don't know. We'll find a way to be together through this."

Willow takes a step back and releases a half-laugh. "How would that work, Reid? What possible scenario do you see where this is salvageable?"

"I don't know, but it has to be."

She wipes another tear from her face. "Okay, let's talk about it. I want a baby. Do you?"

"No, the Fortino bloodline has to end with me and Leo."

"And what about marriage?"

My mind reels as I try to find the words to make her understand why I don't want to ruin *us* by getting married. But all I say is, "I love you, Willow."

"You love me, but you don't want to get married, and you don't want to have a baby. So, basically, you want me to be a permanent girlfriend?"

"I want you to … to be … in my life," I stammer. None of this is coming out right. "There is no one else that matters to me like you do."

Her eyes pool back with another round of tears. "But I don't matter *enough*, right?"

"This isn't about enough. This is about me not being able to be a husband and father, but not wanting to give you up. I love you too much."

She nods. "So then you'll be okay with me having a baby on my own in the next year or so, using a sperm donor? You understand that becoming a mom is what I've always wanted, and if you can't give it to me, another man will provide the thing I want most in this world?"

Fuck no. "No. I know that makes me sound like a caveman and whatever, but I can't stand the thought of another man inside you in any way. I can't watch … I can't see or … think about that."

"So where does that leave us?"

There's a loud ringing in my head right now and I'm ready to lose it. She knows why. She heard the stories, and that wasn't even the half of it.

My gaze is locked on Willow, the woman I love more than anything. She's beautiful, smart, funny, and makes everything better. My entire world is a better place because of her, and I would destroy that if we got married. The darkness that my family possesses would tarnish her.

What about when we fight and more of my father becomes prevalent? What then? How will I ever live with myself knowing that I came from a man like him and ruined her? I can't have a baby, because the cycle will continue.

Another male Fortino to further distort the world.

No. No fucking way.

"I won't have a child. I don't want to get married not because I don't love you but because I do love you."

She closes her eyes, letting a tear slowly drip down her cheek. "I know. I know that's what you think at least."

"But you asked me anyway?"

"I gave you the only option I could think of to keep us together." Willow's voice is low. "You can't handle me having another man's baby, no matter how clinical it is. But you won't have a baby with me, or give me the things that I want and need, which leaves us here."

"Where is that?"

Her hand lifts as she runs her fingers through my hair. "At the end."

"Willow," I say quickly and step back. "Why can't you give us more time?"

She laughs once. "Time for what? Time to drag me along,

make me fall further in love with you, while you wait me out until I can't have kids?"

"No, I want you to have what you want. Of course I do."

"You just won't be the man to give it to me."

Jesus. She doesn't get it. "You don't really want it to be me. You can't want what my mother has lived with her whole life! I won't do that to you, Willow. I won't allow you to become a shell of the woman you were because I've drained the life out of you. I won't make my kids deal with the hell that comes from having a Fortino as a father. And … fuck, I know I'm not being fair to you," I say as the fight drains out of me. "But I'm asking you to be happy with what I can give you, take me for who I am."

The realization hits me like a brick—I'm my father. I'm selfish and unforgiving. Here I am, standing here, begging her to love me unconditionally, but not willing to love her the same way.

"You are not your father, Reid. One day, you're going to see that. *I* see that."

If only that were true. I'm him in many ways, she just doesn't see it. I was groomed by him to be a complete replica. My job, my life, was all laid out for me, and while I might have walked away, his blood is still there in my veins.

"You see hope for change where there's none," I tell her.

"You're wrong. But you know what? I can't fix this. I can't force you to see yourself clearly, and I refuse to give up everything I've ever wanted."

I start to pace, desperate to find something to make this situation different. She has to understand it's not about keeping her from what she wants, but about protecting her from what would come.

"Willow, please, just listen to me." My heart is racing. I see the goodbye. I know exactly where this is going. "If we can just stay like this, we'll be fine."

"No, we won't. I'm always going to know there's an expiration date. You can't want that for me."

I don't want any of this. "Give me a year."

"And then, what, Reid? Huh? Then you walk away?"

"I don't know!" I yell and grip the back of the chair. "I don't know, but I can't fucking lose you, Wills."

She takes a few steps back. "You can't give me what I want. I can't give you what you want, and staying for a year or two, or even a few *days,* is going to lead to the same result."

"You knew this. You knew how I felt about marriage and kids. You knew I couldn't give you this! Now I'm the bad guy?"

Her head shakes and tears keep falling, each one slicing me open. "You knew what I wanted too. You knew before we ever slept together that I was going to have a baby. We both entered this relationship with eyes wide open, but thinking … God, I don't even know what I was thinking."

I do. I know exactly what it was. Like every other woman alive, she thought she could change a man. However, that couldn't happen here because I will never hurt her by doing what I know would only injure her. "I guess that's it then."

"I guess that's … you guess that's it? It's that easy for you?"

"None of this is easy, but I can't change your mind and you sure as hell can't change mine."

She drops her face into her hands and cries harder. I want so badly to comfort her, but I can't. I don't want to make promises I can't keep. Even though it kills me to see her in pain—especially knowing that I'm the one hurting her—I can't give in on this.

"You're breaking my heart," she sobs.

It's another knife through my chest, the biggest one yet, but I don't pull it out. "In the end, the people you love always do."

Then I turn around and walk out of her kitchen, out of her apartment, out of her life.

>———♡——→

I slam the door to my apartment and go directly to the fridge to grab a beer.

"What's wrong with you?" Leo asks from his spot on the couch.

Without answering, I twist off the cap with an angry jerk of my wrist and tip up the bottle.

"Did you and Willow have a fight?"

"I don't want to talk about it," I snap, then drink again.

"Okay." He goes back to his bag of popcorn and movie.

But suddenly I *do* want to talk about this. Leo would understand, right? He'd agree that my having kids would be the worst fucking decision I ever made. He would know that there are people who were meant to be fathers and people who were not. He and I did not get the good dad genes.

"She's completely out of her mind," I say.

My brother glances at me. "I thought you didn't want to talk about it."

"She lied to me."

"She did?"

"Yes. She told me she canceled that appointment at the fertility clinic, but she didn't."

Leo ponders that. "Huh. Kind of unlike her. To lie to you, I mean."

"I might not know her as well as I thought I did." I take another long pull on my beer. "For example, I never thought she would be the kind of girl to think she could change me. I thought she understood who I was and wanted me anyway."

Leo stands up and ambles over to the counter with his popcorn bag. "What does she want to change?"

"She wants me to be the kind of person who can be a dad. And I'm not."

He shoves a handful of popcorn in his mouth. "She wants you to be the dad of some other dude's kid?"

"No." I drink again. "She asked *me* to be the father."

Leo's eyebrows shoot up. "No shit."

"No shit. It's ludicrous."

As he chews, he appears to think hard about it. "So how would that work exactly? Would you be the guy that jerks off in the lab or would you just have sex the regular way to get the kid?"

"It's not going to work at all, Leo, because I said no fucking way! I don't want to be a father at all, with or without Willow!"

"So was she mad?" He shovels another fistful of popcorn in his mouth.

"Yes, she was mad. But she's got no right to be. I never lied to her. I never led her to believe I wanted kids."

"But you knew that she did," he points out.

"Yeah, but that seemed like something she would do way in the future. I don't understand why she can't just be happy with me for now!"

He shrugs. "Girls are always thinking ahead. There's this chick I work with at the store who's like nineteen, and she has her wedding all planned out already, like right down to the dude's Batman socks. She just doesn't know who the dude is yet."

I shake my head and finish off my beer. "Girls are ridiculous. They've been sold this fantasy of perfection—perfect guy, perfect wedding, perfect life—and none of it's real. I know, because I use their devotion to the fantasy to sell shit to them every single day."

"So did you guys break up or what?"

"Yes." I set the empty bottle on the counter and grab a second beer from the fridge. "She wants the fantasy and I'm too much of a realist. I know what marriage does to people in our family. I've seen it—the expectations are too high, and the disappointment and resentment are inevitable. You end up hating each other, even if you stay married."

"Are her parents divorced?" Leo asks.

"No, and that's another part of the problem. Her parents somehow make it look easy. They're like the one in a million couple that figured it out. Willow thinks it can be like that for everyone, but it can't."

"Maybe it can be that way for you guys though. You could try."

"There's no point, Leo!" I yell, angry that he's taking her side. I don't know why I even bothered to tell him anything—he thinks like a child. "And I refuse to watch us self-destruct the way I watched Mom and Dad. It's too painful."

Before Leo can say anything else, I grab my beer, march over to the couch and flop onto it. "We're done."

CHAPTER TWENTY-THREE

Willow

SOMEHOW I GET MY ASS OUT OF BED THE NEXT MORNING. My eyes are so puffy they feel as though they've swollen shut, but I have to function. I can't lie around here because everything I look at reminds me of Reid. His scent clung to my pillow as I slept, making me yearn for him. When I took a shower, all I remembered was him climbing in there, making me dirty and then washing me clean again.

Then when it's time to grab breakfast, I see the insane amount of food in my fridge and start crying all over again.

Fuck love.

When I get to the office, I brace myself for some sort of platitude about what the universe wants or advice on how to cleanse my chakras. Instead, when Aspen sees me, the look on her face says it all.

"I'm sorry," she says softly and then comes over, wrapping her arms around me in a crushing hug. "I'm so, so sorry, Wills. I hoped that you guys would've found a way to survive this."

"Thanks." I'm struggling not to cry, and it's tough. "It didn't work the way either of us hoped."

"Want to talk about it?"

"Not really. Maybe once the pain subsides a little. Or at least when it doesn't feel so raw." Which basically means never.

She releases me and nods. "You let me know when you're ready. I'm here for you."

The lump in my throat grows bigger. To fight off tears, I decide to focus on moving forward. "I could use your help with something."

"Anything," she says.

"Want to help me choose a donor for insemination? I brought the profile book with me. If I can choose one by the end of the week, I might be able to start the first cycle next month."

"Of course. This is my niece or nephew we're talking about here. I'm going to be their favorite babysitter, aren't I?"

I glance at Aspen's outfit for the day—it looks like she's fashioned a skirt out of recycled paper bags—and feel a twinge of nervousness. "Uh, sure."

We sit down at the small conference table with cups of coffee and go through all the profiles in the book, but I have a hard time feeling enthusiastic about it.

"So what color hair and eyes do you want?" Aspen asks. "Do you have a preference for ethnicity? Ooooh, I think you should have a Ukrainian baby!"

"Why?"

She shrugs. "I don't know, it just sounds cool. Hey, what about this one? He sounds great." She reads aloud from the page. "Tall, dark hair with blue eyes, with an Italian background."

"No."

"Why not?"

"Because Reid is tall with dark hair and blue eyes. He's Italian, and if I can't have Reid, I sure as hell don't want to look at a baby that will only further remind me of him."

Aspen nods once and releases a heavy sigh. "Right. Makes sense. No Italian, got it."

She continues to flip a little further. "Oh! Look at this guy! Artistic and quiet with a calm demeanor. Mellow and approachable. Likes nature and cooking. Of German, Norwegian, and French descent." She smiles at me. "No Italian blood, and the total opposite kind of personality."

I check out the profile of Donor #4347. When I look at all the information, I just want to throw the book. I don't care what the guy is like because he's not the guy I want anyway. "I don't know. I can't think."

Aspen touches my hand. "Wills, you don't have to do this now, you know? You're dealing with a lot."

"No, I'm just dealing with a reality that I never should've gone after Reid in the first place. I knew he didn't want what I did, but I deluded myself into thinking I was enough to make him see how wrong he was."

"You are more than enough."

"Not for him!" I say, and then an onslaught of tears fall. "I wasn't enough for him, Aspen. He didn't love me enough to even consider it. He didn't mull it over, it was just 'no.' It wasn't this slug it out and find a way, it was give up the baby and keep him—knowing I was never going to be more than a girlfriend—or give him up and have a child. I had to choose … and … and I can't do this! I just wanted him to love me."

She pulls me to her, and I break apart. All of the emotions

flood me like a tsunami with one wave after another. Each one drags me under and when I catch my breath again, another hits. I'm trying so hard to keep afloat, but I'm drowning in the pain of losing him.

There are so many questions.

Why didn't he love me enough to even try?

Why did I think this would work?

Why couldn't he leave the door open for the future?

Why can't I give up what I want for him?

How the hell do I live without him?

"You can do this," she assures me. "I know it doesn't feel like it, but I know you can. You are so strong, Willow."

I look at her, wishing I could believe that. Right now, I don't feel strong. "I wanted him so much."

"I know."

"I would've been patient with him. I would've shown him just how amazing he is, but he's just so hell-bent on avoiding anything that reminds him the slightest bit of his father that he's basically ensuring that he'll live a life just like him—lonely."

"You can't change people, Willow."

I know she's right, but I can't help but feel like this is my failure too.

If I meant that much to him, wouldn't he have even tried?

"And you shouldn't have to change for him. You wanted a baby long before Reid," Aspen continues. "Giving that dream up would've crushed you. No matter what pain you're in now, that would've been a wound that never healed."

"I guess." Fighting more tears, I sit back in my chair, shoulders slumped. "It's going to be so hard doing this without his support. I never imagined myself going through it alone."

My sister looks offended. "You're not alone, Willow.

You've got me, you've got Mom and Dad, and you've got friends other than Reid. We'll all support you."

"Thanks, Aspen." This has to be one of the most intense and productive conversations I've ever had with my sister. Usually they're filled with strange ideas that are totally off the wall.

"Of course. Look, it won't be easy, but you are never alone. Reid was important in your life, and losing him will inevitably suck."

She has no idea. He wasn't just important, he was everything. I spent all my time with him. He knew everything about me. He was my *person*. And that was *before* we fell in love. "Yeah. It's really going to suck."

"Do you want to look for that prize sperm?"

I want to look for a dark cave to crawl into. I want to go back in time and stand my ground. I want to find his parents and knock them upside their heads.

Aspen claps her hands and squeals. "Look, here's one who likes yoga and camping, and he makes his own jewelry, clothing, and leathercraft!"

I laugh as I sniff back the remainder of my tears. "I don't like any of those things."

She stares into space for a moment. "True. Maybe I should have a baby with him."

I roll my eyes. "Look, Aspen, I changed my mind. I'm not really in the right headspace to choose a donor yet. Let's give it a few days."

"Okay. Suit yourself."

I go back to my desk and try to keep my mind off Reid by clearing out my inbox, listening to voice mails, responding to inquiries, and setting up client interviews, but it's hopeless.

By lunchtime, I'm so miserable I can't even be at work anymore.

I make some excuse to Aspen, which I'm sure she sees through, and go home early. Back in my apartment, I put on my pajamas, wrap myself in a blanket, and curl up on the couch with a box of tissues, a pint of Chunky Monkey, and a Jane Austen marathon on TCM. But even Mr. Darcy doesn't make me feel better. And Willoughby ... God, Willoughby just crushes what's left of my soul.

How am I ever going to get over losing the love of my life and my best friend in one crushing blow?

»—♡—→

The following afternoon, I'm still lying on the couch in a vegetative state when I hear a knock on my apartment door.

I didn't even attempt to go to work this morning. Sleep was fleeting last night, and when I did finally get rest, my dreams were filled with a little dark-haired, blue-eyed baby boy.

Needless to say, that dream will never come true.

The knock sounds again.

I don't care who it is. If it's Reid, I have nothing to say. If it's Leo, I don't want to see him. If it's my sister, well, I'm not in the mood.

"Leave it at the door."

"I will not." The voice is probably the only one that can make me move. "Open this door right now, Willow."

"Give me a second, Mom."

I look around the apartment and know there's nothing I could do to cover up my misery. There are candy wrappers, empty ice cream containers, and chip bags on the table. I'm in the same clothes I wore yesterday, and God only knows what my face looks like.

Whatever.

I keep the blanket around me as I shuffle to the door and open it. "Hi."

"Oh, dear God," she says as she enters. "Your sister told me what happened."

"Good, then I don't have to explain it."

"Can you explain why you're not at work?"

I look at my mother in her crisp black dress with a pair of red heels and the beautiful pearls that hang on her neck. She's the epitome of class and poise. I've always admired that about her. She must be looking at me right now wondering how I came from her.

"I'm dead inside. That's why I'm not at work."

She sighs. "You're not dead inside. You're hurting, and I'm sorry for that. No mother wants to see her little girl in pain."

I shake my head while falling back on the couch. "Stupid love and my stupid heart. Stupid boys and their stupid inability to see what they have. I should've stayed single, so I wouldn't have to struggle like this."

"Did you think it was going to be easy, Willow? Did you think your heart couldn't be hurt when you fell in love?"

"No," I admit. "I knew it could hurt."

"It can also be healed, darling. But it won't heal itself."

"What would you like me to do, Mother? Reid walked out."

She walks over, kicking the tub of ice cream, and scoffs. "So you're giving up?"

"Instead of what? Begging? Am I supposed to keep stabbing my own heart for fun?"

Mom falls quiet, taking in the scene around her and then looks at me. "Perhaps you're right, Willow. Perhaps I was the one who was mistaken."

"What does that mean?"

"It means," she says, her voice softening, "maybe I was wrong when I matched you with Reid. I thought I saw something there, but ... perhaps it wasn't real."

Now it's my turn to be shocked. "Matched me with Reid? But you had nothing to do with ..."

Oh my God, she did. I can't believe I didn't see it. My mother orchestrated the entire thing. Maybe it wasn't on purpose at first, but there she was, the puppeteer in our little show. She made me have to be the one to match him, knowing there were feelings we were ignoring.

"What were you saying?"

"How? Why? What the hell were you thinking?"

"Isn't it obvious?" Mom folds her hands in front of her. "I was thinking that you both had very deep feelings for each other and that together, you'd both get what you wanted, but I was wrong, Willow. I'm very sorry."

"What exactly did you think we both wanted?"

"Well, you wanted a family, and whether Reid knows it or not, so does he. The visions are the same even if the pathways were different. He didn't know what love looked like, and you, my sweet girl ..." Her hand cups my cheek. "You're practically a never-ending supply of unconditional love. You wanted a husband and kids, and I hoped you and Reid would see the happy future you could give each other. But he just wasn't ready for it, and I don't know that he ever will be. There's a very deep hurt inside of him. Until he's ready to heal it, he'll never be able to accept love."

A tear falls down my cheek. "And what do I do? How do I force him to accept love?"

"You can't. That's something he has to figure out on his own."

"What if he never does?"

"Then you move on." She takes my hand. "Is a family still what you want? Even if it means you have to give up Reid?"

"Yes." The word slips from my lips as another tear slips from my eye.

I want to move forward in my life. I'll never love another man like I love Reid. There won't be a replacement for him. No one will ever be able to live in his shadow, and that's the one thing I have to come to terms with. He will always be my great love. I just wasn't his.

"Then, you have to let him go and not let losing him cost you anything else."

"You mean the baby," I say.

"I mean that if you gave him up because you were ready to have a child, then why would you put that off? Unless it's not what you want anymore, but that's something only you can decide." My mother gets to her feet as the words make my chest tight. "I came to bring you this."

She hands me a piece of paper folded in half. I open it up and it's a message from the clinic to call them and on the bottom is Aspen's chicken scratch with the number 4347.

I look up at my mom who gives me a sad smile. She leans in and kisses my cheek. "Nothing in life is perfect, sweetheart. It's all a matter of priorities and timing. I'll see you in the office tomorrow … take today and clean yourself and your apartment. Don't let your dreams die over a broken heart."

Easy for her to say, she's never suffered through one like this. "It just hurts so much."

"I know, and I hate that you're in pain. But I would also hate to see you let your dream opportunity pass you by ..."

I don't want my dream chance to pass me by either. My cycle is due in a week, and I would be able to start after that. But I have to make a choice. "I don't want losing him to be for nothing. I know that I want this baby, and clearly Reid isn't going to be the man to give it to me. But I'm scared."

"No matter what you choose, Willow, I'll be here."

"Thanks, Mom," I say and then sniff because I thought the same about Reid.

She heads to the door, opens it, and then looks back at me. "I'm sorry if my pushing you and Reid together caused you pain, sweetheart. I really thought that you two were going to be a perfect match."

My eyes well with tears. "There's no such thing as perfect. We were imperfect from the start."

CHAPTER TWENTY-FOUR

Reid

I'T'S BEEN A REALLY SHITTY DAY. NOT THAT THERE'S BEEN A good day since Willow and I broke up. Each day is just one more step down on the descent into hell. I keep waiting for it to get better, but it doesn't.

Tonight, I had a dinner meeting that ran later than expected, not that I have any big reason to rush home, but I haven't slept in three days and I'm fucking beat. Now, it's almost nine and I'm just getting to the building.

The only high point is that Leo has improv class, which means I don't have to listen to his unwelcome relationship advice. It would benefit us both if before he spoke, he remembered he lives with me thanks to his last fuck-up of a relationship, but then he wouldn't be Leo.

I grab the mail from the box and get in the elevator, brooding as I flip through the huge stack. I asked Leo to pick up the mail this week, but clearly he ignored me.

Bill. Another bill. Oh, look, more fucking bills, and a greeting card with no return address.

I start to open the card, curious as to who the hell sent me something, when the doors start to close. Before they do, I hear someone yell and a hand reaches into the space between them. "Hold the elevator!"

And the shitty day I was having just hit rock bottom.

It's Willow. She gets on the elevator and stands there, blond hair in a ponytail, wearing a pencil skirt, white blouse, and a pair of running shoes. The cause of all my misery, sleeplessness, anxiety.

She's fucking beautiful.

More beautiful than my worthless mind has been recalling every goddamn minute.

She's just ... more.

"Oh." Her soft voice squeaks as her eyes meet mine. "Sorry, I can just take the next one."

As much as I'd like that because being trapped in a small space with her will be my equivalent of hell, I attempt a lazy smile and chuckle. "Don't be ridiculous, Wills. We're going to run into each other."

She bites her lower lip and looks down. "Right. Okay. We'll just rip the Band-Aid off now so it won't hurt later."

She says that as if it's just a scrape.

That's not what the loss of her is. No, this is a big, gaping, raw, open wound that stitches can't hold together. It's as though a part of my body is missing and it hurts, but I don't tell her that. "Exactly."

Willow leans against the wall on the opposite side. We start to climb, and I swear to God this is the slowest elevator in the city of Chicago. I don't even think we're moving. The silence in here is uncomfortable and you could cut the tension with a knife.

She's right here in front of me. I could touch her if I just reached out a little. I clench my fists to keep myself from doing just that because I don't have that right anymore. Willow Hayes isn't mine. She wants what I can't give her and what I don't deserve.

Instead, I get to just look at her and hate myself a little bit more. I wish I could see her eyes, though. The way she used to look at me could be enough to hold me over for a few hours at least. Her smile might give me a whole night of peace.

I deserve at least that, right?

"So," I say, waiting for her gaze to lift.

And it does and my chest fucking aches. "So ..."

Get knocked up yet? Decide you don't want kids and you'll come back to me? Are you okay after that asshole you fell in love with turned out to be a douchebag?

"How's work?" I ask.

Her lips part and she stares at me for a second. "Umm, it's fine. What about you?"

I'm miserable and a bear to work with. I hate myself. I hate you for making me love you. I hate people, the sun, food, breathing. "Great. Things are good. Work is going well and I'm just staying busy."

"That's great," she says and then looks back down. After another few seconds, she looks back up. "How's Leo?"

"He's Leo."

"Well, tell him I said hello."

I look up and we have two more floors to go. Suddenly, it doesn't feel like time is moving too slow, it's going at rapid speed. She's going to walk out and go to her apartment and I'll be in mine—alone. I want to rush forward and hit the stop

217

button. Tell her I love her and I need her. Beg her to understand and give me time, but it won't be fair.

We'll never see eye to eye and I won't be the man that breaks her.

"I will."

The elevator dings and the doors open. And my heart is pounding. I don't know when I'll see her again, hear her voice, get even a glimpse into her life. This is what our relationship has been reduced to … me praying I can be near her in the elevator.

We both stand there and I step forward. "Go ahead."

"Thanks."

This isn't us. We're not indifferent strangers. Before, she would've just walked out or her arm would've been hooked in mine. We would've kissed the entire ride up just a few days ago. If I went back further, we would've been laughing and smiling as we made fun of our siblings or griped about our jobs.

I guess this is the new us. The people we once were are gone because we never should've tried when we were doomed from the start.

We get to the doors of our apartments, and feeling shittier than ever, I can't hold back. This can't be the way it is because that would be the saddest thing. Not only that, I *need* her. I don't care that we have differences, we're fucking Reid and Willow, the unbreakable friends that everyone else was jealous of. There has to be a way. "Hey, Wills …" I call her name as she stands in front of her door.

She turns. "Yes?" Her eyes are so trusting, hopeful, and I see everything I want right here.

The hope is what does me in. She still thinks there's a man

worth more inside of me. Someone who is capable of loving her and giving her more than what I can. It's false and it brings me to my knees. "Have a good night."

Her eyes close as she nods. "Yeah, you too."

There's not a chance in hell that will happen. There's nothing good without her.

I can't stop thinking it.

As I rummage through the pitifully empty refrigerator—there's nothing good without her.

As I sit staring at a stupid, sappy movie on TV—there's nothing good without her.

As I lie awake in bed, contemplating thousands of lonely nights like this—there's nothing good without her.

Is this really what my life is going to be like from now on? Day after day, night after night of missing her? Of hating myself for letting her go? Of wishing I could be someone else?

Why does it have to be so fucking hard for me to imagine myself as a husband and father? Deep in my heart, I want to be those things for her ... but I'm scared. I have no idea how to be the man that she deserves.

And yet I love her enough to do anything for her, don't I? Even face off against my own monsters under the bed? Look them in the eye and tell them to fuck right off? Banish them from my life forever so I can not only make Willow happy, but be happy with myself?

But how?

I lie awake for hours until it hits me out of nowhere—I know what I have to do.

>—♡→

Early the following morning, I go straight to my father's office. It isn't even eight yet, but I know he'll be here already.

I hardly slept last night but feel oddly energized as the elevator rises to the twenty-second floor of the downtown Chicago skyscraper where The Fortino Group's executive suites are housed. My pulse is racing, and my stomach muscles are tight. My hands clench repeatedly at my sides.

The administrative staff isn't in yet, so I'm able to walk right past reception and his assistant's desk, and barge into his swanky corner office with a view of the lake. My father sits reading a newspaper at his desk, cup of coffee in one thick-fingered hand. He's wearing a dark suit, red tie tightly knotted, salt-and-pepper hair neatly combed back. He has a broad chest, a prominent brow, and a granite slab of a chin. If not for the expensive clothing and cufflinks, he might look more like a mob boss than a CEO.

He looks up from his desk in annoyance at the intrusion. "Reid? What the hell?"

"I want to talk to you."

"Then make an appointment."

"I'm your son. I shouldn't need an appointment to talk to you!"

He sits back in his chair and studies me. "What's this about? Have you come to your senses? Are you ready to quit picking around at that stupid little job working for someone else and take your place here?"

"There's no way in hell I'd work for you."

His dark eyes turn beady. "You've got something against money, power, and success, is that it?"

"I've got something against the man who destroyed my family."

"When are you going to grow up? You're a Fortino, for fuck's sake. Act like one." He's getting riled up, and I find myself enjoying it. As a kid, his temper scared me, but I'm not afraid of him anymore.

"You might think I'm a Fortino, but it's only in name."

"It's in your blood."

I shake my head and realize something for the first time. "You're wrong. My blood is my own. And I'm tired of feeling like I'm being punished for your mistakes. I'm not you."

He cocks his head to one side. "Is this some kind of sins-of-the-father bullshit? What the hell are you talking about?"

"I'm talking about the fact I might have just lost the best thing that ever happened to me because I was too afraid of being like you."

He looks amused. "Are you talking about a girl?"

"I'm talking about Willow. She's not just some girl—she's everything to me, and I walked out on her."

"And somehow that's my fault?" His smirk infuriates me.

"Yes!" I snap. "Because she wants a good man—a *real* man, a man who'd be a good husband and father. And thanks to you, I have no fucking idea what that looks like!"

"Listen, you're smart to ditch the girl now, whatever the reason. Marriage is a hassle no man needs. An impossible game to win."

"It's not a game at all, Dad. It's real life, and the way you treated Mom had real consequences—for her, and for Leo and me. Your game playing wrecked our entire family. Why do you think mom drinks so much? Why do you think Leo can't hold a job? Why did I grow up being more of a father to Leo than you ever were?"

Riled up, my dad gets to his feet. "Your mother expected

too much—it fucking exhausted me! And your brother was a spoiled brat who never toughened up and grew a backbone. He's been a pansy his entire life."

"Don't talk about him like that!" I move forward and lean over the desk to get in his face. "All he ever wanted—all any of us ever wanted was to feel like we mattered to you! But you were too self-centered to care."

"A man provides for his family, and that's what I did! Christ, did you think your privileged life was free? The million-dollar house? The cars? The vacations? The Ivy League education? And how about the trips to rehab? You think those are cheap? I've had to work for every cent, Reid."

"We could have lived with less money and more attention."

He rolls his eyes. "So you'd have been happier being poor? What a joke. You're wasting my time, Reid. If you didn't come here to take your place in this company, then what the hell do you want from me? I can't turn back time, and even if I could, I am who I am, and I'm not going to change. Your mother knew who she married."

I look at him for a long, hard moment over that desk, and find relief when I see no trace of myself in his face. "I don't want anything from you anymore. I came here today to confront you, to ask you why you treated us all like dirt, like possessions—as though we didn't mean as much to you as the fancy cars in your garage. I wanted to look you in the eye and say *fuck you* for never being there. Fuck you for not caring more. Fuck you for making me feel like I can't be a better man. Because I can. And I will."

We stare at each other for a few more seconds, and even though we're the same height, I feel taller than my father for the first time. Bigger. Stronger. More powerful.

"See you around, Dad." Without looking back, I stride out of his office and down the hall to the elevator.

I feel like a million bucks, like a huge weight has been lifted off me, like I've let go of something that's been dragging me down all my life. There's still work to do, of course, but I'm not scared of it.

I know what I want, and that's a life with Willow.

I just have to figure out a way to get her back.

CHAPTER TWENTY-FIVE

Willow

THE DAY AFTER I RAN INTO REID IN THE ELEVATOR feels endless. It's Friday, but the prospect of the weekend means nothing to me anymore. There's no hope of anything being fun without Reid.

I work late, desperate for the distraction, and walk home about seven, pulling my coat tighter around me in the chilly autumn darkness. In my shoulder bag is the slip of paper with Aspen's writing on it—number 4347. All day long, I kept thinking of picking up the phone and making the call, but I couldn't bring myself to do it. I want it to feel fun and exciting, and right now I'm incapable of those feelings.

First thing Monday, I promise myself. That's when I'll call.

In the lobby of my building, I hold my breath as the elevator doors open. I don't want to see him and have to cross paths, wondering where he's off to on a Friday night. What if he's dressed up for a date? What if he's freshly shaven? What if he's wearing cologne? The thought of him preparing to spend time with another woman makes me insane with jealousy.

But the doors open, and he isn't there.

I'm both relieved and disappointed. I miss his eyes and his smile and his hands and his smell and—just everything. Being in the elevator with him yesterday was torture.

The doors open on my floor, and the hall is empty and quiet. With a heavy sigh, I make my way toward my door. While I'm standing there digging out my keys, I can hear the TV on in Reid and Leo's apartment, but the weird thing is, I hear music coming from mine. Did I leave something on?

Frowning, I put my ear up to the door, and sure enough, I hear Dean Martin crooning away in there. What the hell?

I let myself in, and the first thing that hits me is a delectable aroma—it smells like an Italian restaurant. Tomatoes and garlic and fresh bread and oregano. My mouth waters immediately, even as my brain tries to make sense of it. Am I on the wrong floor?

Panicked that I somehow managed to let myself into the wrong apartment, I glance around, but the furniture is mine.

That's when Reid comes out of the kitchen, carrying a board full of charcuterie. "Oh! You're home! I didn't hear you come in."

I stare at him, dumbfounded. He's wearing an apron over his button-down. It's red and says CAUTION: Extremely Hot.

"What are you doing?" I ask him.

"Cooking you dinner." He walks over to the coffee table and sets the board down next to an open bottle of wine and two empty glasses I hadn't noticed before.

"Why?" My heart has started to pound. Is this for real?

"Because we're celebrating." He comes around the couch and takes my hands. "At least, I hope we are."

"Reid, I'm feeling a little lost here." I shake my head. "What on earth would we be celebrating?"

"The future. Our future."

"We have a future?"

"Of course we do." He presses his lips to mine before I can stop him. "And in our future, I make meatballs for you!"

"Wait a minute, wait a minute." I shake off his hands and move away from him. "This isn't okay, Reid. I've spent the last week drowning in tears because you walked out on us. You can't just waltz in here with meatballs and Dean Martin and make it all better. Someday maybe we can be friends again, but I'm not there yet."

"I don't want to be friends, Willow." Reid moves close enough to take my face in his hands. "I want more. I want it all. And I want it forever."

I'm almost scared to ask, but I have to. "What do you mean, you want it all? What's *all*?"

"I want to be all the things you deserve—a husband, a father, the love of your life." He kisses me again. "I love you, Wills. I can't go one more day without you."

Behind him the room is spinning. "But what about what you said before? I thought you never wanted to get married or have kids."

"I didn't think I did. But I think a lot of that was fear—I was scared I'd fail and you'd end up hating me, resenting me for everything I'm not. But I'm not afraid anymore."

"You're not?"

He shook his head. "No. Because even though I know I'm not perfect, I'm not my father. You were right. I don't think like him, and I'm not doomed to make the mistakes he made."

"No," I say, tears making his face go blurry. "You're not. But how do I know you're really ready to commit to a future with me? I'm done fooling around, Reid. I'm ready for the next stage of my life to begin. How can I trust that you are too?"

He takes me by the shoulders, his expression serious. "I know you're scared, and I don't blame you. If you've been half as miserable as I have this week, you never want to go through this again. But I'm asking you to give me a chance. Let me prove to you that I mean what I'm saying. That I can make you happy. That I will be the man you want me to be."

All of this sounds perfect. It's what I've hoped, prayed, and dreamed he'd say all in one fell swoop. And while he might not be scared, I sure as hell am. "I can't endure losing you again," I confess as a tear falls down my face.

"Believe me, Willow, I can't handle the idea of it either. I was a fucking basket case."

"In the elevator ..."

I don't want to remember it, but it was utter agony for me. I wanted to rush into his arms, take the comfort of my best friend, but he was the cause of the pain.

"What about it?"

"You were fine!"

He shakes his head. "I was the furthest thing from that, Willow. I was a coward, but I wasn't fine. But in a way, I'm glad I had to see you. It made me see everything so clearly. Looking at you, being that close to you, but not being able to have you was too much. I'd had enough of being ruled by my past."

"How did you figure all this out?"

"I saw him."

"Who?"

"My father," he says as he takes a step closer. "I went there. I wanted answers from him. I needed to know why he was such a piece of shit and a coward."

"Did he tell you?" Another tear falls. I imagine him standing there, asking his father to explain himself, knowing how hard that must've been.

"That's the thing." Reid captures my face in his hands. His eyes are full of emotion as he looks down at me. "I didn't care about those answers anymore, Wills. I got the answer to the only question that mattered and it didn't even come from him."

"I don't understand."

"It came from you. The way you looked at me. The way you smile. The way you're strong in your convictions even when it meant walking away from me. You would never become my mother and I am nothing like my father."

A sob breaks from my chest and Reid pulls me tight in his arms. As he holds me, my world starts to piece itself back together. "I told you," I mutter and he chuckles.

"I know you did. I wasn't ready to hear it. I will never treat you like he treats my mother. Our kids won't have to wonder if I love them because it would never be in question."

"Tell me this isn't a dream." My eyes meet his again and even through the blurry tears that continue to fall, I see the honesty there.

He wants this. He wants us. Not some half-assed relationship—he wants it all. Reid slayed his dragon so he could come back and win me.

"No, sweetheart, it's not a dream. But I have one more thing …" Then he takes my hands in his and drops to his knee. My eyes are wide and my heart is racing.

"Reid …" I say, giving him the out because he has to be out of his mind.

"I know I don't deserve you. I know you're better than me in every way. I've lived the last seven days without you, and I never want to live another one like that. I want to wake up beside you, kiss you, make love to you. I want to give you the family you want. There will never be a day that you don't know how much I love you. I want to watch you walk down the aisle, give you as many kids as you want, and grow old beside you. So I'm asking you Willow Hayes, will you marry me?"

My heart is pounding as I stare down at this man I love with my whole heart. This is everything I've ever wanted to hear and nothing I thought I ever would. "Yes," I say, and then inhale, trying to hold it together. "Yes, yes, yes!"

His smile is triumphant as he gets to his feet. He pulls me to his chest and then his lips are on mine. Our mouths move together, and my fingers hold his face to mine. I wasn't sure I would ever do this again. I thought it was gone forever, and now, I don't think I can stop.

I love him so much it hurts.

Reid puts me back down and breaks the kiss. He steps back, reaching into his pocket. "I got so swept up, I completely forgot this part." He pulls out a little black box. "This wasn't a kneejerk reaction. You see, I was walking back after my talk, knowing that you were the only thing in the world I wanted and when I looked up, I was in front of a jewelry store." He opens the box, showing me the stunning pear-shaped diamond ring nestled in the velvet slot. "I looked in the window and there was this ring. I didn't hesitate one second. I knew right then it was meant to be on your hand."

I try so hard not to cry. I've done so much of it, but I'm so overwhelmed. "Reid …"

He removes the ring and takes my hand. "I never believed in love before you, Willow. It was this myth that people told themselves to feel better about their lives, but then you gave me your heart, and I realized that *I* was the one living a lie. I don't want that anymore. You're my truth, and remember …" Reid smiles as he pushes the ring over my knuckle. "You already said yes."

I reach up, touching my hand to his cheek, the light catching the diamond, sending prisms around the room. "You really are perfect."

"I'm only perfect because I have you."

EPILOGUE

THAT WHOLE THING ABOUT GROOMS BEING LATE FOR their weddings is crap, as far as I'm concerned. It's the bride who's late for mine. We should be married already!

I'm standing here with Leo—who is no damn help—like a fool, shifting around and pretending I'm not being impatient.

I look back up at her parents' lake house, wondering what the hell is going on. It's not like she didn't get here on time—we slept here. Well, sleeping wasn't really what we did.

Sure, we started off in separate bedrooms—she wanted to play the role of the virginal bride on her wedding night, but when I snuck in and woke her up with my head between her legs, she didn't kick me out. I quite enjoyed the rest of my night.

Aspen comes walking up with an uncomfortable smile. "Hey, so she'll be just a bit longer."

I smile back and talk through my teeth. "What is taking so long?"

She turns her back to the people sitting in the blistering sun so she can talk. "Well, her dress isn't fitting right thanks to the fact that you knocked her up, so she's in tears."

"Tell her I'm baking out here."

"I would, but she probably doesn't care, so you're going to have to be a little understanding."

I square my shoulders, rather proud of the fact that just three months into our engagement, we learned that she was pregnant. We weren't really trying to do it or trying to stop it. It just happened, and I was thrilled about it. I proved my male prowess without needing to stick a turkey baster anywhere near her.

I am man, hear me make baby.

Aspen rolls her eyes. "You can tone down your testosterone there buddy, we get it, you did your manly duty. Pride and all that is beaming from your aura."

No matter how much time I spend around my soon-to-be sister-in-law, I'll never understand her. "I made her happy."

"Yes, good job."

Leo snorts. "At least he can do one thing right."

I turn and smirk at my brother. "I definitely do that right."

"Yeah, we've all had the pleasure of overhearing it too."

I don't even feel bad about that. Willow and I love sex, and that's not a bad thing. Come to think of it, I'm shocked we didn't get pregnant sooner. Once we got back together, we were going at it all the time.

"Oh, Jesus," Aspen groans. "You're practically glowing red now. Can't you two keep yourselves in check? I made a mention of you before and she lit up like a Christmas tree."

"Nope. When you love someone, that's sort of how it goes."

"Says the new expert on love?" Leo laughs once.

"As much fun as this is," Aspen interrupts, "I'm going to check on my very pregnant and uncomfortable sister. You should … entertain the crowd or something. I would suggest not discussing your sexual abilities, since my Aunt Louise might have a heart attack."

"How the hell am I going to do that?" I ask.

"I don't know, think of something."

She's off before I can say anything else, smiling and waving at what was supposed to be a very small group of people. We thought maybe twenty people, but it's over a hundred sitting here staring at me. Willow's mother wasn't having it any other way.

When she found out we were having a baby, Willow regretted that choice since there is no denying it with her very prominent bump. She's seven months along and absolutely radiant.

"I'll do improv," Leo offers. "My teacher says I'm totally ready." And before I can stop him, he's in the center of the aisle.

"Hey everyone! I'm excited to be here with you today. My brother is marrying Willow, which you all know, but in case you made a wrong right turn on your way to someone else's wedding …"

Crickets.

Oh, I'm going to die for this.

"Tough crowd." He chuckles. "I met Willow a few years ago when my brother let me come live in his apartment, which I guess is now my apartment, since he's moved out. I've known Reid since, well, since the day I was born. Since he's my brother and all …"

Dear God, this is why he's broke. It's time to take matters into my own hands before my brother is booed out of my wedding.

"Okay," I say and clap Leo on the shoulder. "Willow is going to be down soon and then we'll get on with the wedding. I know it's hot, and you're all sweltering, but just give me a few minutes and I'll be right back. Try not to kill the entertainment, it's unpaid."

I head up the aisle and into the house. After climbing the stairs two at a time, I hear her voice.

"He's never going to want me!"

"Willow, stop, you're being crazy, of course Reid will want you," her mother tries to soothe her.

"What's that saying? Why buy the cow when you can get the milk for free? I'm an entire herd of cows, and he's going to take one look at me and run away."

I never understood the guys at work who would talk about their pregnant wives being irrational. It made no sense how a woman that was perfectly normal became someone else, and now I get it. The hormones make them fucking crazy.

Well, I can handle crazy, I was born and raised in that. What I can't handle is her thinking that I don't want her.

"Not a chance of that, Wills," I tell her as I open the door and look at her. I know we're not supposed to see the bride before the wedding, but I snuck out at six am this morning, so I think that ship sailed.

However, nothing could've ever prepared me for this moment. She's stunning. Her long blond hair is in some kind of twists and curls down at the base of her neck. She has a lace veil that frames her perfect face, and she rests her hands on her swollen belly over the robe she's wearing. Willow is absolutely breathtaking.

"Run away while you can, Reid." She sniffs and turns her back to me.

"Only place I'm running is to you, so get your gorgeous ass down there and marry me."

"Just go away."

"Not a chance of that."

Her tear-filled eyes meet mine. "I can't zip my dress. I can't marry you if I don't have a dress."

"I don't care if you're naked. We're getting married today."

She shakes her head and points at her stomach. "You did this."

"Damn right I did."

"Well, I'm not going down there naked. No dress, no wedding."

I walk over to her, cupping her face in my hand. "Willow Hayes, that's the last time that name will ever be used. I don't care if you're wearing a bedsheet, nothing is going to stop me from making you my wife today. If that means I get the priest up here and I marry you in this bedroom, then so be it."

A tear falls down her cheek. "You still want me?"

As if that's a question. "Always."

"Even now when I'm fat and puffy?"

"You're not fat and you're not puffy. You're perfect."

I wipe the tear as she lets out a laugh. "You're blind, but I'm glad you are."

Aspen sniffs. "That was the sweetest thing ever, and you're in luck." We both look over as she holds up a white sheet. "I happen to make clothes, and I can fix this."

"Oh, Jesus. My sister is going to make my wedding dress?

I give up," Willow grumbles and I pull her to my chest with a chuckle.

I look over at Aspen. "You have five minutes and then I'm coming back in here and marrying her with or without a dress, got it?"

Aspen grins. "Consider it done. Now, let me work my magic."

I head out of the room, check my watch, and run down to check on Leo. This may end up being a small wedding after all once he scares off the guests.

When I get out there, I hear them all laugh. Leo is actually working the crowd. He's smiling, telling them some sort of story, and at this point, I just have to pray it's not about me. Then I take a second to see how happy he is. He's at ease, and there's no sense of the doom that usually follows him around.

It makes it just a little easier, knowing I'm leaving him on his own. Although, that's not really true either, since he'll be across the hall and I'm still paying his rent. He's like a teenager I can't get rid of.

When I get back inside, the door opens before the five minutes are up. Aspen emerges first, pushing against my chest. "Oh no, buddy, you already saw her once, you're not seeing her in the dress. Now, go back to your spot and wait."

"You fixed it?"

She grins. "I did. She's right behind me, in her dress that fits now, and there's no more tears." *Thank God.* "Now, go!"

Practically sprinting back outside, I give Leo a thumbs up and he stops talking. The music cues a minute later and the bridal procession starts. First her mother, then Aspen after her, and I've never been more grateful that we at least kept this part small.

I look down at the grass, wanting to savor the moment when I'll see her for the last time as Willow Hayes, my best friend, my love, my everything.

Slowly, I lift my gaze, and when I do, I can't breathe. My heart swells and tears blur my vision. God, how could she become even more beautiful in five minutes? How could she manage to steal my breath so easily when I just saw her?

Everything fades away, except for her.

Her smile is soft as she walks toward me. Then she stops, her brown eyes shining with so much love it humbles me beyond words.

"Hi," she says.

"Hi."

"Do you like the dress?"

I don't even see the dress. Is she wearing one?

"I love you."

Willow releases a quiet giggle. "I love you too."

"Good thing since we're getting married."

She squeezes my hand. "Thank you."

"For what?"

"For giving me everything I ever wanted."

She has no idea how much she gives me. All I want is to make her happy and prove each day that I deserve her. I bring my free hand to her face, wiping the lone tear that rests on her cheek. "No, Wills, it's you that did that for me, and I will do everything I can to deserve it."

She smiles at me, and our new life together begins.

BONUS SCENE

Willow

"**I**'M A HIPPOPOTAMUS," I MOAN, STARING AT MY 41 weeks pregnant self in the full-length mirror in our bedroom. I'm wearing one of Reid's white T-shirts, the only thing that's comfortable to sleep in these days, and even that is stretched to within an inch of its life. I turn to the side. "My belly looks like a watermelon under this shirt. Not even a regular-sized watermelon. A watermelon with a pituitary problem."

"Come to bed," Reid says. He's already stretched out beneath the sheets. "I'll make you feel all better. I love your body, melons and all."

"You can't love this body. There is no way." Shaking my head, I face myself straight on again and put my hands on my belly. "Why won't he come out already? Why does he have to be late? I'm a punctual person. I'm never tardy." I give Reid a dirty look over my shoulder. "He must get it from you."

Reid laughs. "Give the kid a break. He's just waiting to make an entrance."

"Also you." I look down at my belly and speak softly, trying to cajole our son into vacating my belly already. "Hi there, peanut. We can't wait to meet you. Don't you want to come out and play with us? See the sunshine? Breathe the oxygen? Get off my bladder?"

Behind me, Reid laughs. "I can't imagine that being too comfortable."

"It's not." Turning away from the mirror, I waddle over to the side of the bed. "Anything you've imagined, add on twenty-five more layers of misery—swollen feet, not that I can even see them anymore, exhaustion, aching back, nausea, heartburn, indigestion, Braxton Hicks, a thousand weird cravings ..."

"You haven't had that many weird cravings," Reid says in my defense.

I regard him with disdain. "Really. You didn't think it was weird when I sent you out at one in the morning to get me some Easy Cheese and powdered doughnuts?"

"Nope."

"How about the pulled pork on top of vanilla ice cream?"

"That one was good, actually."

"And the Twinkies dipped in ketchup?"

Reid winces. "Yeah, that one was a little strange."

"And I didn't even tell you about the time I was tempted to spoon dirt onto my Cinnamon Toast Crunch. I was too embarrassed."

"Dirt is a very common pregnancy craving, Willow. You don't need to feel shame about it, and you certainly don't have to be embarrassed in front of me. I'd love you even if you'd eaten the dirt."

"You would?" My heart melts a little bit. I really do have the best husband ever.

He nods. "Definitely."

I smile and gesture toward the spot next to him. "Got room for a Willowpotamus over there?"

"As a matter of fact, I do," he says, turning down the blankets.

I get on the bed and crawl past him to my side of the bed, slipping my legs beneath the sheet. Reid props up the pillows behind me the way I like and covers me to the waist—or at least where my waist used to be.

Then he scoots down, lifts the T-shirt I'm wearing, and kisses my belly. "Hello in there," he croons. "Why don't you come out now and give your hot mama a break?"

"Reid!" I scold. "Don't call me a hot mama in front of him."

"Why not? It's true, and it will always be true, and I'm not going to pretend my wife isn't the hottest woman in the world just because my kid is in the room."

I sigh and play with his hair. "You're hopeless. But I love you."

"I love you too." He palms my tummy with one hand, fingers splayed, and puts his lips right next to my skin. "And I love you, little dude. I can't wait to meet you."

The baby responded with a few digs of his heel. Lately he couldn't even kick anymore, because there was absolutely no more room. I groan, trying to shift my weight into a more comfortable position, but it's hopeless. Everything hurts. "He hears you," I tell Reid. "Keep talking to him. Maybe he'll listen."

"Maybe it's because we don't have a name for him yet," Reid says, looking up at me. "I think we should decide."

"I thought we agreed to wait and see what he looks like," I protest. Reid and I did not agree on names.

"He's going to look like a baby. Don't they all look alike?"

"No!"

"They do to me."

I sigh, shifting my weight again. My hip joints are killing me, and it feels like pain is radiating from my tailbone. "Okay, what are your current top three?"

"Bruce Wayne, Thor Odinson, and Oswald Cobblepot."

I roll my eyes. "Be serious."

"I am being serious. The comic book universe is a treasure trove of baby names."

"Well, so is English Literature."

Reid wrinkles his nose. "Those names are boring."

I smack his shoulder. "They are not! They're classic. And I like the idea of using a last name as a first name—it makes it more modern. Jane Austen has plenty of potential options."

"Like what?"

"Well, like Darcy."

"No fucking way." He looks at my belly. "Sorry about the f-bomb, Bruce."

"How about Churchill?"

He shakes his head.

"Willoughby?"

"That's even meaner than Oswald Cobblepot."

"Pemberley? Fairfax? Knightley?"

Reid closes his eyes and snores.

"Parker?"

Reid picks his head up. "I like that. Spiderman's real last name was Parker."

"I know. And it's got that classic sound too."

"Parker what? Like what would his middle name be?"

I shrug. "I'll give a little on that if you want to go more comic book. But not Cobblepot!"

"Lee? For Stan Lee?"

"Parker Lee Fortino," I say, trying it out. "I kind of like it."

"Parker Lee Fortino," echoes Reid.

And right at that moment, my water broke.

"Oh my God." I grab my belly. "Oh. My. God."

"What?" Reid says, lifting himself onto one hip and looking at me with concern. "Are you okay?"

I stare at him in disbelief. "I think I'm in labor. Or I wet the bed. But I think it was my water breaking!"

Reid goes white as a sheet, and for a moment I'm scared he might panic or even pass out, and I need him to be my rock through this. I'm prepared—I think—but I'm scared too.

But then he jumps out of bed and starts racing around the room, tearing off his pajamas and throwing on random clothes. "Okay. I'm ready. This is good. I'm good. Got pants on. Got socks. Got a bag all packed and ready to go." He pauses to look in the mirror and smooth his hair back before grabbing the small suitcase in the corner of our room. He's halfway to the door when I yell, "Reid!"

He looks over at me in surprise.

"Aren't you forgetting something?" I pant as a contraction hits me.

"What?"

"Me!"

"Oh my God!" He drops the suitcase and rushes to my side. "I'm so sorry, Willow. I don't know where my head is. I'm all flustered."

"It's fine," I tell him, swinging my legs over the side of the bed. "Just help me to the bathroom and bring me a change of clothes, okay? And my phone."

"Okay."

Twenty minutes later, we're in a cab on our way to the hospital.

"Well," I say, laughing a little now that I'm in a lull between contractions. "Guess you were right about the name."

Reid kisses my hand. "Do you really like it?"

"Yes. And I think he does too. Don't you, Parker?"

Our son responded by moving even lower in my body.

"Oh God," I groan. "I hope we don't hit any traffic. This boy knows what he wants, and he wants out."

"Don't worry, baby. We'll get there fast." Reid knocks on the partition. "Hurry, please. We're in labor back here."

"He knows, Reid. We told him like five times already." I pat his leg. "But thank you."

At the hospital, I'm checked in quickly and given a private birthing suite. The nurses get me undressed and settled in bed, and soon afterward the doctor comes in.

"Finally, huh?" she says with a grin. "Let's see how you're coming along."

After the exam, she tells me she thinks it will be another six to eight hours, but this baby is definitely on his way. I'm terrified at the thought of another eight hours of this pain, but one look at Reid and he immediately comes over to take my hand.

"You've got this," he says quietly, his expression loving and determined. All traces of his earlier nerves are gone.

"Don't leave me," I beg.

"Never." He squeezes my hand. "I will be with you every step of the way."

And he is—through the awkward exams and the intense contractions and the unimaginable pressure and almost unbearable pain of bringing our son into the world. He holds my hand and speaks softly. He wipes sweat from my brow and cheers loudly. He tells me I am strong and beautiful. And when he holds our baby in his arms for the first time, he cries tears of pure love and happiness.

"Hi, Parker," he croaks, his voice cracking. "Hello, little man."

I'm crying too—from the overwhelming joy and pain of giving birth, from the sight of Reid cradling a child with such tenderness, from the knowledge that I'm actually a mom now, from exhaustion, from relief, from a heart overflowing with love and gratitude.

He looks up at me. "You did it," he says softly, his eyes filling again.

"We did it," I tell him. "Bring him closer. Let me see."

Reid moves tighter to my side and holds Parker so I can look at his pinched, mottled little face and sparse tufts of dark hair. "He's perfect."

I smile. "Spoken like a proud dad."

"I am proud." Reid leans over and kisses my lips. "Of both of you."

"I think he looks like you," I tell him. "He's got your eyes."

"But he has your little nose," says Reid. "And that dimple in your chin."

I laugh a little. "You're right, he does."

"God, Willow. I didn't think it was possible to love anything this much." He looks down at our son in awe, and his expression is almost fearful. "I had no idea."

"You're going to be a great dad, Reid."

He nods. "I'm going to try."

"I love you."

"I love you too." He kisses me again, and his smile lights up my world. "And this is only the beginning."

ABOUT THE AUTHORS

New York Times, USA Today, and *Wall Street Journal* Bestseller Corinne Michaels is the author of nine romance novels. She's an emotional, witty, sarcastic, and fun loving mom of two beautiful children. Corinne is happily married to the man of her dreams and is a former Navy wife.

After spending months away from her husband while he was deployed, reading and writing was her escape from the loneliness. She enjoys putting her characters through intense heartbreak and finding a way to heal them through their struggles. Her stories are chock full of emotion, humor, and unrelenting love.

USA Today bestselling author Melanie Harlow likes her martinis dry, her heels high, and her history with the naughty bits left in. When she's not writing or reading, she gets her kicks from TV series like *VEEP, Game of Thrones,* and *Homeland.* She occasionally runs three miles, but only so she can have more gin and steak.

She lifts her glass to romance readers and writers from her home near Detroit, MI, where she lives with her husband, two daughters, and pet rabbit.

ALSO BY MELANIE HARLOW AND CORINNE MICHAELS

Co-Written Novels

Hold You Close

Imperfect Match

The Salvation Series

Beloved

Beholden

Consolation

Conviction

Defenseless

Evermore: A Salvation Series Novella

Indefinite (Coming 2019)

Inseparable (Coming 2019)

Return to Me Series

Say You'll Stay

Say You Want Me

Say I'm Yours

Say You Won't Let Go: A Return to Me/Masters and Mercenaries Novella

Second Time Around Series

We Own Tonight

One Last Time

Not Until You

If I Only Knew

Co-Written Novel with Melanie Harlow

Hold You Close

Imperfect Match

Books by Melanie Harlow

The Speak Easy Duet

The Frenched Series

Frenched

Yanked

Forked

Floored

The Happy Crazy Love Series

Some Sort of Happy

Some Sort of Crazy

Some Sort of Love

The After We Fall Series

Man Candy

After We Fall

If You Were Mine

From This Moment

The One and Only Series

Only You

Only Him

Only Love

The Cloverleigh Farms Series

Irresistible

Undeniable (Coming May 2019)

Strong Enough (A M/M romance cowritten with David Romanov)

ACKNOWLEDGMENTS

From Corinne Michaels… To my husband & kids: I love you guys so much. You put up with the worst of me and still find the best hidden beneath the layers of stress. I don't know how I would survive without you.

Melanie: First, thank you for doing this again with me. You have no idea the joy that working with you has brought me. I laugh, smile, and anxiously await whatever form of punishment you will give me for my last send back. I will never be able to adequately explain the gratefulness I have that we started this journey. Your friendship means the world to me.

Christy: Thank you for always being there for me, listening, and understanding whatever it is I need. I love you even when I hate you.

Sommer: You're the best. You seriously took a photo and made it into one of my favorite covers ever. Melanie and I love how you just get us.

Nicole: I fell in love with that image and I'm so beyond happy that we were able to use this for this title. It's truly perfect.

To my friends: I know I'm often distracted and a mess and I'll never be able to thank you for loving me regardless.

From Melanie Harlow... To my husband and daughters, it's because you bring so much love and laughter to my life that I'm able to write happily-ever-afters. You're everything to me.

Corinne: Thanks again for a million laughs (and hardly any tears this time around)! My good witch would be boring and tedious without your bad witch to bring out her mischievous side. I appreciate the incredible gift for storytelling and gut-punching you bring to this partnership, and I'm so grateful for your trust in me. You make me better. And one day soon, we are going to have cocktails together for real!

Melissa and Brandi: You're a dream team. You make my life easier and more fun every single day!

Jenn and the SB Team: Thank you for everything you do for us!

Kimberly: A million thanks for putting our stories into the hands of readers all over the world.

Nancy: Once again, thank you for saving us from a book full of tense errors, weird ellipses, missing words, confusing sentences, and mysterious changing eye colors...

Janice, Melissa, Michele, and Yvonne: Thanks for reading early and being our eagle eyes!

To our readers: we love you and hope you had as much fun reading this story as we had writing it! Join our reader groups on Facebook and let us know!

Made in the USA
Middletown, DE
02 January 2024

47108421R00141